Pseud Ambofilius

The marriage of time

A rhymed story

Pseud Ambofilius

The marriage of time
A rhymed story

ISBN/EAN: 9783337262136

Printed in Europe, USA, Canada, Australia, Japan

Cover: Foto ©Andreas Hilbeck / pixelio.de

More available books at **www.hansebooks.com**

THE
MARRIAGE OF TIME.

A RHYMED STORY,

BY

AMBOFILIUS.

TINSLEY BROTHERS,
CATHERINE STREET, STRAND,
LONDON.
1881.

COLSTON AND SON, PRINTERS, EDINBURGH.

P R O E M.

—•◇•—

WALK in, fair Reader, and peruse my
    lines ;
Be patient when you light on what's
    amiss,
And don't forget, when my poor Muse
    declines

Facile consilia damus aliis.

THE MARRIAGE OF TIME.

———◆———

WHEN I set out to join this expedition,

The age I lived in had grown slow and prosy;

So fearful slow indeed, I thought a mission

To stir up the world and make things rosy

Was laudable; for, of all grave pursuits

That folks engage in to fill up their days,

There is nothing bears so few and little fruits

As each repeating what the other says.

In truth, Imagination looks like dead.

George Eliot's gone: where have we now a head?

A

For, look ; or listen ; What d'ye see or hear ?

Say, what is there to-day or writ or said

To cause a man to laugh or shed a tear ?

The times have changed since Shakespeare

          charmed the age.

Where have we now a poet, whose great name

Shines forth upon the world's broad stage

Like the great William's of surpassing fame ?

Says one, ' I'll wager I can find his match ;

I'll bet, and lay a thousand pennies on.'

' Done !' says another, who is quick to catch

Advantage ; 'I know ! you mean Tennyson.'

' Bah !' says a third ; ' is that the man you mean ?

He has ideas, and they are fine sometimes ;

But they are few and very far between.

Yet he's the Laureate of our fruitless times.'

' Well, there's Browning : what do you think of

　　him ? '

He is a poetic Wagner, so profound ;

So full of poor ideas to the brim,

That all who try to find his wit get drown'd.

Like the famed German of the Nibelung,

He can't or won't be simple ; which is it ? '

Germans *must* be obscure ; their songs are sung

In a loose way, just like their breeches fit.

Bob Browning, though, *has* bones in his longlines;

You seem to see him twist and turn about,

And rub and polish, till it all so shines

That even *he* can't tell what it's about.

There are the Morrises, who rant and bawl ;

William, of Earthly Paradise, to wit ;

Who draws designs for papering your hall,

And in between makes rhymes that do not fit.

We've had of late some poems through nine

      editions,

Which some one said were pleasing to the ladies ;

'Tis nothing but *réchauffé* inspirations,

Which he prenomens ' Epic of Hades.'

In poetry one surely ought to try

For some new theme ; to be so weak as

Always on Greek or Roman to rely,

Makes the poor reader feel he must reply,

O imitatores, servum pecus !

Young Algernon deserves a place, of course !

The name of Swinburne's something by itself.

His Pegasus is fleet, but rather coarse ;

Some of his lines are better on the shelf.

Perhaps his sunrise songs should be perused

Before sunrise, when one is better able

To comprehend the sense.   For when one's

    snoozed,

One's clearer than fresh from the supper table.

Across the ' Straits ' they have a poet, 'tis true,

A Frenchman to the pith of his backbone—

There's no denying he's a genius too ;

Like a great pyramid he stands alone,

A very Jupiter in power.   He flies

Across the realms of Fancy plucking flowers

Of language, whose rich perfume never dies ;

But for all time sheds fragrance in full showers.

To poets, we may say, wherever you go,

You will find the poems of Victor Hugo.

The greatest of Republics owns a son

Whose songs will fill the world when he's long
          dead ;
Of all those millions he's the only one
They have produced with a poetic head.

To go from poetry to sober prose,
What find we there to raise man's thoughts
          from earth ?
Your daily 'leading articles ?'   Heaven knows
How deused few of them are twopence worth !
Your Quarterly and Edinburgh Reviews
(With articles on subjects worn to thread,
And not the smallest particle of news)
Are out of date, and long since should be dead.
Of magazines the country has enough
In all conscience ! What shall we do with more ?
Those that appear are filled with such poor stuff !

(The authors think, of course! it's learnéd lore)

We have curious evening papers, every day,

For little money and with much less news.

We've journals Liberal and organs Tory;

Each wears its spectacles of red or blue,

And colours thus the little daily story

Of its politics, which often is not true.

The proletariat *Echo* leads the way;

It's read by those who live in slums and mews.

Next, the pink *Globe*, like a dandy daughter,

The oldest of them all, but not the best,

Looks as if some tippler's brandy-and-water

Had been spilt beyond the tippler's vest.

For years we've had a paper called *Pall Mall*,

Whose editor much loved to overthrow

Opponents. But, poor man, himself he fell,

As cocks do sometimes when they overcrow.

He jumped up quickly and soon crow'd again,

Adhering pluckily to his old ways.

He stabbed his foes regardless of the pain

He gave.   I doubt if the new stabber pays.

Who reads them ?   That's the problem I can't

    solve :

Chiefly the needy authors, I suppose ;

For, he who reads one would, I am sure, resolve

He would on no account repeat the dose.

We have some writers, though, right mighty men !

There's Ruskin, who is rather curious ;

But he's done wonders with his facile pen ;

Of late his style is rather furious.

He writes on paintings, though he does not paint,

And finds effects the painters did not mean ;

And when you say he's wrong, he says he ain't ;

He'd say it in a minute to the Queen.

Of weekly organs there is one *Spectator*,

Like every organ, with its set of tunes.

He ' grinds' on Saturday, this arch-dictator,

On Monday it's all forgot.   If he impugns

The motives of the Saturday Reviler,

An altercation of six months ensues.

This, people like; 'tis hardly, though, the style a

First-class journal its readers should amuse.

A so-called social organ's come to life ;

A worse abomination than the rest ;

They pry into the secrets of your wife,

And really are a most infernal pest.

Fors clavigera is very funny

Sometimes.   He poses for a Solomon.

The Jewish king had more in him for the money,

Although our Friend is not a hollow man.

In science we have some *quasi*-learned heads.

There's Huxley, who they say stands first, for

place.

He's fond of your plesiosaurian beds

And descants well on every extinct race.

Then Owen comes with megatherium head;

He won't believe in what he don't find out,

Which is not much to make a fuss about.

For him and Spenser to be in one bed,

When some kind friend had blown the candle out,

Would be the grandest fun. They are daggers

drawn.

Owen declares that Spenser is quite wrong

To say, when prehistoric man was born,

That he'd no legs and could not walk along.

Of all this tribe who revel in old bones,

And have an insight into things gone by,

The diamond among these precious stones,

Is Darwin Charles.   His penetrative eye

Has seen through more in his good spell of life

Than all the rest together have found out.

He says man's instinct takes the prettiest wife,

And pigs, like men, admire the finest snout.

Two idle navvies passing down Cornhill,

Saw in a shop Charles Darwin's photograph.

'He says we've come from monkeys, I say,
　　　Bill;'

'No wonder!' says the other, with a laugh;

'Of all attempts at perfect human shape

That natural selection has turned out,

There's nothin' nearer the gorilla ape

Than that 'ere pictur' (followed by a shout).

In   painting,   well !   we've   some   good   men ;
    but hush !
They are very sensitive about applause ;
If you find fault with Millais or his brush,
He'll call you names and other things, because,
Like Leighton, Watts, and all the big R.A.s,
He is used to being lauded and adored.
He does not think that sometimes the hurrays
Come from admirers inwardly much bored.
The purity of art is, we much fear,
Being damaged by your Whistlers, and that lot ;
The age we live in is an age of beer,
And painters mostly paint to boil their pot.
A meretricious style of painted story
Is now *de rigueur*, and by some admired ;
But work like that of Gustav Doré
Makes judges sigh and feel very tired.

Another type of man this country owns,

A pupil of Rossetti, also good.

His name sounds not like Raffaelle, 'tis Burne

     Jones ;

His reputation's high, though, and its stood

The test of critics, enemies, and friends.

This painter won't run with the common herd ;

He 's independent, and his way he wends

In silence ; waiting ; saying not a word.

In other walks where intellect 's required,

Is the work better done ? for I'm afraid

The quality's gone off ; 'tis being hired

People think of, and still more of being paid.

The real truth of the position is,

Your great mobocracy is too well fed ;

Genius is work, and work diminishes

When people eat too much and lie in bed.

What is it, then, in which this age excels,

If art and literature and music declin ed ?

I think I hear the answer from your 'swells,'

Who've breakfasted at twelve and lunched
and dined.

'Tis brewing, babbling, boasting of big bets

Wagered with Tories born plutocratic ;

Who, with plundered pounds, fawn upon their
pets,

The ' hard-up ' landowners aristocratic.

We have a few, 'tis true, good men with heads,

Whose jaws, by Jove ! Dame Nature has well
greased,

Poor fellows ! For they're never in their beds

Until the cock has crow'd and Parnell's pleased

To hold his jaw. Statecraft's our modern art !

Each shopman knows as much as Beaconsfield

About your politics, for which one grieves :

Your great snob mob can act too well that part,

As the great statesman we have named believes.

He thinks they're too much power allowed

      to wield.

In these great times of travel what d'ye see

From morn till night, and all the long night

      through ?

The horse of fire and steam speed tremblingly

With thousands o'er the iron road, a crew

Of Pleasure seekers : That's the modern god !

Verbum sap. ; erat demonstrandum quod.

'Twas at the period when the iron road

Had spanned our earth and brought all nations

      near,

That the Avenger Time was roused. He showed

To an observant eye, that wear and tear

On him, as on the rest of living things,

Had done its work, and half destroyed his wings.

'Confound my age! Time always should be

       young,'

He said.   'The verdure of the early spring

Should not surpass the freshness of Time's wing.'

With this reflection he turned round and sung,

To cheer himself, a favourite ancient song,

Which he had, many a thousand years ago,

Heard angels singing as they marched along.

He thought he saw them marching row and row

In legions, white and golden, reaching far

Into the heavens, each shining like a star.

His memory brought him back the harmony

Of their accorded voices, as it fell

In dulcet strains and rose to fuller swell,

With solemn march of measured minstrelsy.

'Twas passing strange, he thought, that he

    should feel

As mortals do, when their three score and ten

Of years have made them shrivelled, shrunken

    men ;

' For Time is surely something much more real,'

Said he, ' than just a mortal's life ; and then,

If I'm to mark the time for worlds unborn,

And show to coming generations here,

That I am none the worse for being worn,

I am bound,' he said, ' to keep each little sphere

In her orbit ; for if Gravitation,

Following Time, relaxed her discipline,

And gave scant heed, what dire devastation

Might such policy entail.   No! I say;

Old Time, like others, must, if he's to win

The good opinion of celestial powers,

Perform his duty ; and in such a way

That he will mark, not only all the hours,

But all the minutes, seconds, and much less

Of Time's divisions ; for your natural brains,

My earthly sons, have reached a subtleness

Through evolution's polish, that measures

In astronomy are like weightless grains,

Indefinite small, to suit the calculation.

The orbs below, as with great Heaven's nation,

Where purer virtues are, and greater treasures,

Must be in order and exact rotation.'

Proceeding with his grave soliloquy,

Time smoothed his hoary locks and changed

    his face.

'Enough!' he said, 'of this cold, lonely life.

Enough! enough! Proclaimed be my decree

To nations, peoples, worlds throughout all space,

That Time, like men, must find himself a wife.

This life's dull monotone strikes cold on me.

From morn till night and night till morn 'tis one

Sad lonesome duty; like the rolling sea

That shifts the sand; when done to be undone,

Like restless billows rising but to fall:

Such is Time's work; and that indeed is all.'

'Bravo! *Probatum est!*' in faltering tones

Slipt into speech, expressing my delight;

But ere the words had left me, all my bones

Right to the pith, were freezing hard with fright.

'The gods ! what have I done ?' I said within

Me.　I'd no pluck to utter more applause—

I really wished my body was so thin

That, like a beam of light, I could his claws

Escape, by slipping through some little crack,

So little that he could not pull me back.

When dwindling life had got a little warm

By waiting till my fright had partly thawed,

I turned my head as slowly as a storm

Begins, when falling on the parchéd sward

The untethered droplets shed their wings and

　　fall,

In cooling moisture at the thunder's call.

I very gently turned, not drawing breath,

Till I the eye of Time could plainly see.

With fear I was so very near my death,

I muttered *Miserere Domine.*

I strained to see, as if I looked through haze ;

Nothing seemed clear except the fearful fog

That held its sway 'twixt Time and my fixed

    gaze,

As objects seem to eyes bedimmed by grog.

' Do speak ! Say something, kill me if you like,'

Scarce audibly I cried, to cause some change.

I felt I would much rather he should strike

My head off, than this way my mind derange.

There's nothing under Heav'n like dead suspense,

Particularly in such company.

'Twas like a lion's cage, whose reddish fence

And teeth-marks tell their tale. Can he

Be such a monster ? Surely I think not.

He moved ; I shivered—' Oh ! good, noble sir,

It's not my fault ; you make my eyes wink hot,'

I said, ' with looking for some sign from you.

Why did you sit so long and never stir ?
You should have spoken.'

    ' What you say is true,'
Said Time with much deliberation ; ' but
I do assure you I was entertained
To that degree, my mouth was tightly shut.
Never did archer, who at centre aimed,
Get his intention home as I have done.
I know you well, my friend ; I know you well.
Perhaps in you I have found the very one
I want.   But what you've heard you must not
  tell.'

' I will keep silence, sir, you may depend ;
But I much wish, if I might be so bold,
To beg of you to be my trusted friend,

And tell me where I am—I feel so cold

In these great halls.'

               ' Ha ! ha ! ha ! ha ! ha ! ha !'

Laughed Time. He said, 'You need not be

     alarmed.

I cannot find you here your own papa ;

But though he's absent, you will not be

     harmed.'

He looked much weather worn ; his flinty pate

Sat rough and rugged on his shoulders broad.

He seemed inclined soon to be intimate,

As if I had touched a sympathetic chord.

He had two wings, from shoulders to the heels,

And a large knife as emblem of his trade.

When he's in bed I wonder how he feels ?

I'll ask him soon ; but now I am afraid.

Such wings in bed are awkward; they might
    crack.

I wonder what he'd do if he were wed ?

He could not anyhow sleep on his back :

Perhaps he'd use them for a feather bed.

I saw no men, or I'd have said, ' How, sirs.

Can you, good conscience ! leave old Time
    like this ?

The Avenger's sitting here minus trousers ;

Supposing *I*, for instance, were a Miss !

In takin him a wife, that makes a pair,

What would she think if she could see him thus ?

He must at church wear something more
    than hair,

Or the archbishops would make such a fuss.'

His dwelling-place was beautiful to see ;

It seemed to be of crystal, all in white.

The heavens all round were visible to me,

All full of stars and suns, a wondrous sight.

While gazing at the many charming things

That filled this lofty hall of Time's abode,

Doors opened and there came with fluttering

    wings

A troop of angels.   Each one showed

That he or she, I could not tell the gender,

Had come express with some important news.

One gave a note,—Time said, 'Who's the

    sender?'

'Please read,' the bearer said, with bows

    profuse.

Meantime the angelic host had filled the place,

And many more of them could find no room.

I had never seen such beauty, and such grace.

Their faultless shapes shone 'neath a golden
    bloom.

Some dark, some fair, all were erect and tall ;

The sign of perfect health dwelt in each eye ;

A matchless concourse in Time's crystal hall.

The Avenger looked at one or two ; the sly

Old fellow thought, I know, of his decree.

Perhaps he'd like to choose one then and there,

And cry out *nupsus sum pulcherrime !*

Some one I've found my loneliness to share.

The note was opened and the meaning read ;

The brows of Time went up as he read down.

' With pleasure, thank you—I will come,' he
    said ;

Upon his forehead crept a little frown.

Retreating then the angelic host took wing,

Their faces smiling like a sun-lit cloud.

They gently marched, then all with instant spring
Were poised on ether, and commenced aloud
To chant again the song which Time had heard
Thousands of years, and more perhaps, ago.

' Listen,' he said ; ' remember every word ;
I love that heavenly song, it soothes me so.'

' Now, Father Time,' I said, ' 'tis evident
You've had enough of celebatic bliss ;
You too like change, and also merriment.
You cannot live without the blissful kiss
That sets man's blood alight and woman's too.'

' Ha ! ha ! you dog ! your fancy is well fed.'
Quoth he, ' You've hit the nail upon the head ;
You read Time's eyes with truth,—I see you do.'

' You see, good Time, I've had experience ;

I have a wife and family at home.

I know love's passion is a wary sense ;

It froths up quickly into fearful foam.'

Time stretched his arms and opened wide his

      mouth,

And gazed from east to west and north to south.

He blew his nose with a terrific snort,

No handkerchief could stand such a report.

' Before to other matters we proceed,

Let me inquire,' said Time, ' if you're agreed,

Who is my worthy friend ?   For I must own

I cannot guess how you came here alone.'

With this old Time pulled up each shaggy brow,

And looked a little anxious to see how

His visitor would answer this request.

He tried meanwhile to look his pleasantest.

What he requested was no more than fair.

I looked about, and thought, and rubbed my
head,

Pushing my fingers through my unbrushed hair.

I stood up straight, and cleared my throat and
said,—

''Tis passing strange, good Time! I cannot
say :

All I know is, I fell asleep one day,

And woke in these great halls, bewildered much.

Don't hurt me, please, for I'm a frail thing.'

Time smiled, as strong men smile, and said,—
' If such,

My worthy friend, is all you claim, Time's wing

Will shelter you, and he will see no harm

Falls on your person ; so composéd be.

Let not your mortal fears feed on alarm.

Here all is peace ; Strife has no lodging here.

Order that's Nature's must in order be

For all time—so be you of good cheer.'

' Much gratitude I feel for your kind words,'

I said.   ' I've heard you wish that you were wed.

Some men and women oft, like whey and curds,

Don't mix well, especially when they're in bed.'

' *Macte virtute ;* you, my boy, are wed.

You are no stranger to a double bed,'

Said Time, high lifting his great hoary head,

And in his face developing much red ;

' But, like most sated sires and *blasé* dames,

You think it wise to hold in check love's flames.

Senses threadbare, like worn vestments, keep

Scant heat in our frail frames; which, as they wane,

Slip one by one life's links till life's asleep,

And like Time's sand has measured its last grain.'

' 'Tis true philosophy Time's mind unfolds,'

I said; ' but wisdom has a feeble growth

In concerns strictly matrimonial.

Like steeds unreined, love's fire its right

      upholds,

Unfettered by laws ceremonial,

To kindle ardour in the veins of both.'

' And you, fair sir, I see, can reason well,'

Said Time,—' Pray let me know your honour's

      name ;

For if the number of my suite you swell,

I must, indeed, of you this favour claim.'

' If that is all the toll I pay, why then,

Most certainly, good Time, I'll soon reveal

What I have had from birth as cognomen.

But one condition I must crave.   I feel,

In joining Time's great suite, from there below

I must be hidden and incognito.

For think, great Time, how much the differ-

ence is

Between one mortal and so great a show

As your grand presence makes.   The sciences,

I trow, will be by Heaven and earth forgot

While such a monster drama holds the scene.

My mother earth will shake.   I know not what

Will be the consequence when you are seen

Joined to a fitting wife by marriage tie.

N e'er has so grand a sight filled human eye ;

Great hallelujahs sure will rend the sky.'

' My worthy friend,' said Time,—' you make

      me laugh—

Ha! ha! ha! ha! ha! ha !   You are full of chaff.

I feel right merry at the thought of this !

Ages on ages have I wandered on,

Through endless space, for countless centuries.

I've thought and dreamed about, and pon-

      dered on

The fate that might be mine, if I were joined

To some fair partner, who my life would cheer.

Why really ! when I think what life might be

With its true ring, like sterling money coined,

It raises me to heights of ecstasy :

Twould change to heaven my lonely dwelling
  here.'

Time stood with outstretched feet and glowing
  face,

And said,—' There is but one of my great race !

'Tis shameful there should be no little Times,

I the big bell and they the little chimes.

I should enjoy my days and morns and nights,

Like mortal men with their own wives and
  sons.

My joy would then reach to celestial heights,

If I like men were blessed with little ones.

O Jupiter ! great Zeus ! rain down on me,

Your oldest servant and your faithful friend,

Your mighty favours ; that my destiny

May be, in time to come, my path to wend

Towards great Creation's altar, where I may

Receive my other half in perfect bliss,

And fold her to my bosom with a kiss.'

' A *carmen triumphale* would be sung,'

I said. 'All Nature would give voice and tune

To swell the great accord; while heaven was
    hung

With blazing suns and many a silver moon.'

' Fair sir,' said Time, ' if my poor suit succeeds,

I'il visit your small globe, and on the range

Of Pelion's mountains crush the dewy weeds.

One foot on Ossa's heights would waken strange

Reflections in the minds of those hard by;

They'd stand and look and rub the astonished eye.

From Alps to Haleakala, on your world,

Would be a morning fly. By Jove! good sir,

A planet could by my command be hurled

And crash its weight against the sister spheres.

Your Himalaya to its utmost spur

This right hand could uproot.   The mountain

   spears

That pierce the snow-clad hills of Jura's chain,

And lift their lofty points to prick the sky,

If Time willed so, could not their place retain ;

But, in his iron grasp must lean and fall

To feed Destruction, and there scattered lie,

Like some great galleon shattered by a squall.'

' Your power of speech reminds me of my home,

Where we have men of wondrous talking

   powers ;

O'er the whole range of classic lore some roam

And sparkle in their talk like meteor showers.'

'Ah! Your home,' said Time; 'that just
    reminds me,
I have not yet been favoured with your name.'

' True,' I said, 'my promise, of course, binds me.
I will tell, hoping I incur no shame.'
Now the time comes at last for me to tell;
Perhaps he finds me all at once a bore.
I wonder, when he hears, if he'll propel
Me from his grand abode, and slam the door.
I felt uneasy, that I must confess;
One does not like to tell one's own affairs
To perfect strangers; who can say or guess
What he may think of doing unawares?
I'm like most others from my faultful world;
The record of my deeds is not pure white—
It can't be helped, the roll must be unfurl'd,

And take its chance, whether half clean or quite.

' My name, good sir, is Ambofilius ;

My father is a minister of state.

He's often told me he felt bilious

When he had to take part in some debate.'

' You have debates to settle your affairs ? '

' Oh, yes !   Our Parliament means chiefly talk.

The greatest talkers get the largest shares

Of what is to be had.   Their daily walk

And daily object and intention, is

To get their family and their best friends

The warmest corners.   Then the pension is

Obtained for him who's prodigal and spends.'

' Does Government,' Time said, ' succeed like

    that ? '

' My father manages to live in style,

He has a very splendid habitat.

He earns his share, I think, without much guile.'

' Who is the greatest talker you possess ? '

' His name is Gladstone, of immense renown.

When he is talking you should see the press

To hear him from all quarters of the town.'

' Say, Ambofilius, what is it he says ? '

' He talks, sir, by the hour ; the shelves are full

Of his political yarns.   He'll talk for days,

And if you contradict him, like a bull

Whose blood has been stirred up with some-

     thing red,

He'll aim a blow with oratory's horns,

And never leave you till he thinks you are dead :

Prick'd to the quick with his mendacious thorns.'

Time here gave evidence of being tired,

And stretched his arms and legs and looked at me.

The idea struck me that he now required

My absence perhaps ; but where was I to flee ?

I turned and looked about and showed to him

That my position was anomalous.

If I had been a female seraphim,

He would, I think, have been most courteous.

Then looking at him with an air of dread

I said, ' I fear that I am in the way ? '

' Oh! no,' he quick replied, and shook his head,

' There is room for many more; now tell me, pray,

If you agree to be Time's willing guest ?

You have come here by some deep laid design ;

You had better make your mind up here to rest,

And for the present blend your fate with mine.'

The great man rose and offered me his hand ;

Huge portals opened and a blaze of light,

Like the mid-day sun on a golden strand

Belting some inland sea, a wondrous sight,

Deluged the spacious hall with golden rays.

I saw no limit to the brilliant show.

Rising and falling endless sparkling sprays,

Crested great waves of fire in ceaseless flow.

We passed the threshold of the entrance door,

And seemed embarked upon a sea of light.

As far as ear could range a gentle roar

Of coruscating cataracts, whose pour

In fan-like spread of silver molten white,

Bathed with a dazzling shine the glowing floor.

The view that lay before us had no bounds

That mortal eye at least could then define.

As we moved on the fringes of faint sounds,

Played tenderly upon his ears and mine.

I strolled along; my feet scarce seemed to touch;

The mortal heaviness had lost its sense.

I felt the soothing of my nerves was such,

That Satisfaction claimed omnipotence.

Our course was lined with servitors, who held,

Some salvers, others goblets filled with wine ;

Some perfumes spread from glowing horns,
       that smelled

Like rarest odour from rare columbine.

Large pendent vessels from an unseen height

Hung motionless, the march of time to mark ;

From which at intervals took silent leave

Drops many hued, drops pink and blue and
 white ;

While now and then, like those who deeply
 grieve,

Was shed one larger drop in colour dark.

No word was spoken ; but my silent host,

His head deflected now and then, to show

What were his wants and what he thought
 were mine.

Of all the things I saw, I wondered most

At the immense expanse.   For row on row,

New beauties dawned in never-ending line.

Far-reaching hills were fringed with orange
 flame ;

High builded temples, made of brilliant stars,

Showed on their tipmost top a fiery name ;

One shone with blinding lustre.   It was Mars.

Ascending an incline, we left behind

The scene we first had entered from Time's home.

The Avenger's palace, with its crystal dome,

Stood out in grand relief.   One saw defined

The crystal pillars and far vaulting spans,

Bridging from point to point as each reclined ;

Upholding their apportioned loads.   No hands

Of mortal, but more sure and subtle brains

Had shed their power and felt the tiring strains

Such efforts must entail.   We   wandered on ;

A heavenly feeling of unmixed repose

Took captive all one's sense. Such glories shone,

One thought alone of joys and banished woes.

The summit reached, a panoramic view

Held vision fast, entranced with such a scene.

Majestic orbs of every size and hue

Reflected all in each ; and in between

An azure vapour, tinted with the beams

Of one great golden sun, enclosed the whole.

' Is this reality, or only dreams ? '

I said, with lifted look.

                 ' My friend, the roll

Of that low thunder that you hear afar,'

Said Time, ' is endless.   'Tis a planet's song.

Before you is creation ; every star

That holds its station, and its place among

Created orbs, is nearer now to you.

Your little planet in its orbit turns

From century to century.   The blue

Surrounding ether, as it slowly burns

With solar radiance, veils the sister spheres,

And makes them seem more distant than they
are.'

' These wondrous beauties rouse my mortal
fears,' I said.

Quoth Time, ' Fear not ! Time rules each star.'

I see no limit to Time's great domain.
If all my dreams of glory were in one,
And with imagination's might and main
Were added to, till splendour was outdone ;
All high conception that my mind has bred
Would, I believe, quite fail to picture more
Than this entrancing scene.   If I were led,
Through some fair angel's choice, to wander o'er
Heaven's majesty itself, I scarce believe

My soul could wider spread with the delight

Which I now feel.   I could from morn till eve,

Unrested in my soul or flesh, till night,

Here stand a gazing statue never tired.

What life must be, good Time, for you in this

Great palace, with your fertile mind inspir'd

With such surroundings ! Sure 'tis perfect bliss,

Though you're alone.   There is no time for care,

Nor for the thought that there is none to share

This glorious paradise.'

                    ' My worthy friend,

I linger on your words ; they warm my heart.

Your mind right well, with good æsthetic bend

Of apt expression, outlines with sure art

The sense I entertain of my home charms.

But Time, as I have said, feels cold alone.'

'There's something wanting as you fold your

arms,'

I said, 'when evening fades, and then is gone.'

' 'Tis true ; your words embrace my constant

thought,'

Said Time.   'I'll marry ; I will change my life ;

Solution of this problem must be sought.

The question is, Who is to be my wife ?

You've feasted, Ambofilius, both your eyes

To such a filling point, that you must be

Content to leave the asteroidal skies

To their own councils, and, my friend, with me

Quit these bright elevated spots, and reach

A lower level where we may commune.

Before we leave, take sight at yonder beach,

There lies Time's vessel in my own lagoon.

We will take ship and spread the ample sails,

And call great Boreas for his northern aid.

We'll sail to south, and if the south us fails,

We'll navigate elsewhere ; for Time has said,

' He'll search and find a wife ; it is to be !

I here proclaim that this is my decree !"

I took a last, a lingering look around ;

My breath welled up within me, as one feels,

When out of silence buds and grows a sound,

Which spreads its fascinating fingers round

The sense of hearing, and quite gently steals

Its force from keen desire.   I loosed a sigh,

And slow and timid, looking upon Time,

Let him perceive that I would say good-bye

To such a glorious, and, in truth, sublime

A place, with fond regret.   He looked on me,

And with a slowly ripening smile, said, ' No,

We must depart.   It is that you may see

And share with me the beauty of the show,

That I propose the vessel.   Let us go.'

Time slowly went before and I behind,

Through groves of heavenly hues full scented

     sweet,

We walk and speak not.   Tendrils of a wind,

Soft with its perfume freight, the senses greet ;

High soaring arches span the shelving way ;

Colours of varied tint, well toned to show

The changing shades, which mantle night and day,

Surround, and warm, and cheer us as we go.

At last the measured step with ceaseless tread

Devoured the distance, and the numerous crew

Of Time's great sailing vessel, which he said

Bent in the waters of his azure blue

And still lagoon, were seen with hurrying steps ;

Some here, some there, quick moving to and fro.

The cordage and the sails in lazy heaps

Lay on the deck ; but one man speaking low

Gave this and that one order, and by slow

Degrees disorder left the ship, and we

The dulcet air of Time's domain caress'd ;

And saw the crouching sails, that were to be

The handmaids of Æolian force when press'd

By Boreas in his wakeful mood, blow out.

' She moves, and we are off !' the seamen shout.

The blazing suns, which threw their radiant glow

O'er Time's domain, now stretched their

  piercing fire.

The ship's good prow seemed delving through

  the flow

Of molten gold and silver. Reaching higher

Than the utmost range of dazzled vision.

Great spires of flame their growing points shot
   out,

Circling round the ship with deft precision,

To light the captain's course as he steer'd out.

The shore of Time's domain grew slowly pale

As all the Boreades spent their power

In feeding full the hollow of each sail.

The sea rose up a crested azure tower

Each side the mighty prow as we sailed on ;

And far behind, in glowing, glistering show,

The sunder'd spray strives hard to fall upon

The Mother Sea, its home down there below.

Time stood upon the spacious deck and gazed,

As one who says farewell to those he knows.

His grand old head and both his arms he raised,

With that strong energy that one, who goes

For ever from his home, will manifest.

He turned to me, and I could see his lip

Was not in his control ; but like the rest

Of his good nature, quivered like the ship.

An impulse stirr'd in me, but I refrained.

The soul itself when troubled 's like the sea,

Whose stately hue is whitened o'er, and stained

By chained emotion, struggling to get free.

At length the misty line that marked the shore,

A wordless epitaph to vanished joys,

Slid into nothing, and was seen no more,

Save in Memoria's glass, which nought destroys.

The farewell ended, and the sorrow drown'd

In thoughts more cheerful, Time said, ' Now,
  my friend,

Good Ambofilius, let us look around ;

Let our eyes search the ship from end to end.

Call here Oceanus, the captain of the craft,

That he may show the working of the gear ;

And store our minds with all, from fore to aft,

Such details as will serve us while we're here.'

Oceanus, with swarthy look, came forth

And through the hairs which armour clad his
      face

Gave omen of a smile, as does the froth

Of teaséd water tossed to mark the place

Where underneath the real meaning lies.

' All hail ! Oceanus.   All hail ! good friend ;

We mark our exit with auspicious skies.'

' 'Tis true,' the captain said.   ' If Boreas lend

His stoutest ether wove into a gale,

We shall the mission of my noble sire achieve,

Without or thought or danger that we fail

Again to reach the charming shores we leave.'

' My heart is warmed with your brave words,'

    said Time.

' Let Boreas and his satellites blow forth ;

For we may have the east or western clime

To visit ; needs may be the south or north.'

So saying, with his eyes Time beckoned me.

Oceanus before us both went down

To see that all was order, and that we

Were wanting nothing that might bring a

    frown

Upon our foreheads. ' This, good sire, for you,'

The captain said, while showing Time the way

To his appointed quarters, which the crew

Had dress'd with trophies ; quite a bright array.

' Good Ambofilius, you will please lodge here,'

Oceanus with pleasing smile then said.

I looked about in case I might feel queer

To see in what direction was the bed.

He saw me look, and broke into a laugh,

As men with sea-brined bowels often do

At pale-faced landsmen ; but I took his chaff

Good humouredly, by myself laughing too.

Our quarters fixed, and other things arranged,

Oceanus gave orders here and there,

To his purveyors of the food and drink,

That they should give due heed to the ship's fare,

And see the daily menu duly changed.

' For,' said Oceanus, ' I'm proud to think

That here, on board, provision 's amply made

For every want ; eat, drink, don't be afraid !'

These comforts looked to and the cabins seen,

The state room next called for a close survey.

Oceanus and Time sat down ; between

Them so invited I took chair, and they

The one and then the other, wished to hear

(Encouraged so to speak by being two)

Of the affairs of my forsaken sphere.

‘ Good friends,’ I said, ‘ ’tis really strange that
      you

Should feel an interest in my little earth.

To such omniscients there is nothing new ;

And what I know, to you is little worth.’

The captain slapt his knees and gently grinned.

Old Time looked on the floor and then at me.

I looked at both and felt the sea and wind

Were undermining my stability.

Oceanus lit up his pipe and said,—

' My friend, let's hear about your greatest men.

I'm very curious.'   He scratched his head.

' Say how you're ruled ; tell of your laws, and
      then

Dilate upon your customs and pursuits ;

What your best people eat and drink, and when

They gather in their harvests and their fruits.'

I must confess I was not very able

To tell them what they wished so much to know.

The servants now began to lay the table,

Which made me feel 'twas nearly time to go.

I tasted something strange upon my tongue,

And thought, indeed ! if I'm not very quick

I shall be late for dinner, for they've rung

The second bell, and I feel very sick.

I waited and kept waiting, as one does,

Pretending that I was in perfect trim.

Each moment I felt iller from the buzz

Of filling the tureens up to the brim

With soup, the smell of which was by itself

Enough to make me sick when on the land.

I put one hand upon the nearest shelf

To help me up, but found I could not stand.

' Now, Ambofilius, keep your pecker up,'

With cheery tones came from Oceanus.

' I'll wager you will like a wrecker sup,

And soon in eating head the three of us.'

Time felt for me, and said in lower tones,

' My good companion looks a little pale ;

Hold up, my friend ! she rolls, you'll break
some bones—

Here, waiter, fetch the gentleman some ale.'

The servant brought the beer up from the hold,

And stood to draw the cork between his knees;

I felt I was much worse and getting cold.

My stomach gave a very awkward squeeze.

At length the crisis came and I ran out,

Or rolled or tumbled, for I don't know which,

And was attended by some stupid lout,

Who somehow let me daub myself with pitch.

With that deliverance over I returned,

And this time steady walked upon my feet.

Oceanus laughed loud and said, ' You've earned

Indeed your dinner now ; come, let us eat.'

Such things for eating as are served at sea

First decked the board.   Imprisoned oily fish

In pungent vinegar were served to me.

I looked and smelled and gently passed the dish,

Preferring something rather less delicious ;

Something hard and dry, a captain's biscuit

Suited best, and, being more nutritious,

Consoled me for the fish.   I would not risk it.

Big bottles, brown and green, appeared anon.

Oceanus could do his share of that.

His glass was filled and its contents were

      gone,

Before I'd time to see what he was at.

The dinner done, and all the things removed,

They called on me to talk of home affairs.

Now that my inside was a little soothed,

I thought I might avoid going down the stairs

To lie down in my berth.   So I began :

' Good sirs, you do me honour thus to wish

That I should things of my own world recount.

I assure you 'twill not be a savory dish.'

'Oh! never mind,' said Time, 'I know the fount

From which your tale will flow is good enough,

I've heard my friend describe such things before,

So Ambofilius now proceed.'

.

                              A puff

Of wind here canted up the floor,

Which sent both Time and me in search of that

Which most resembles what they call a plane.

I vowed I could not without something flat

To stand upon, begin.   She rolled again.

'In my small world, good sirs, we've Parliament

In two divisions, peers and common men.

The commons every now and then are sent

To be exchanged for newer blood, and then

If what we call a good majority

Backs up the Tories and turns out the Whigs,

The Tory chief claims his priority

And takes the reins of power with his colleagues.'

' You have a Queen, I think ? ' said Time,

                                      ' Oh ! yes,'

I said ; ' the best of monarchs, pure and true ;

The greatest potentate on earth ; no less

Is her position.'

                          ' Indeed, and then are you,'

Said Time, ' a people much renowned for work ? '

' In some respects my nation takes the lead.

We've many nations, German, French, and Turk,

Russian, Spanish, Italian, Dane, and Swede ;

We've Chinese, Japanese, Hungarian, Pole,

Fin, Yankee, Tartar, Irishman, and Greek.'

' You've aborigines as black as coal ? '
Oceanus inquiringly remarked.

' I'll speak
Of them in turn ; you must give me a minute.'

' Your nigger,' said Oceanus, ' is sleek :
To get the body whiter you should skin it.'

I thought the captain showed unusual cheek.
Time gave Oceanus a nudge and said,—

' Now, Ambofilius, pray proceed and tell
Us how the people of your earth are fed ;
The things they eat and drink, etcetera.'

'Well,

I've said we have a Queen ; she heads the State.

The Prince of Wales comes next with his

      Princess ;

Princes, Princesses, dukes both small and great,

With their inheritances more or less.

We've lords and ladies, peers with coronets,

Some simple misters who these honours give,

And barons by the gross and baronets,

Scarce one of whom knows how the others live.

They live in houses and go out to walk,

In day-time eat, and in the night they sleep.

Much time is wasted in the smallest talk,

And those who waste it most the longest weep.

Each nation has a town its capital,

Where mostly flock the money-making folks ;

But thousands live without a rap at all,

And think their cleverness the best of jokes.

We've men who, like my father, guide the State,

And when they're out translate Thucydides.

Like other hives we've drones who vegetate,

Preferring of all things decided ease.'

' Much eating and much work don't coincide,'

Oceanus remarked, for he knew well

' The harder worked, the quicker go inside

The worker's meals ; so that you need not

    tell.'

' Oceanus,' said Time, ' should write a book.

Philosophy, indeed, is his strong point.'

Oceanus felt flattered, and his look,

Appreciative movement in the joint

Of his capacious jaw, displayed.

'Well, then,'

I said, 'we've iron things that run by steam,'

Which made Oceanus sit up and stare.

'We've ships that move against the strongest

stream.'

At which Oceanus began to glare.

'We've guns which at one shot would sink this

ship

And many more besides, if they were there.'

Oceanus then bit his under lip,

And on their ends commenced to stand his hair.

'We put one wire all round our little earth,

And touch a handle when we want to talk.

In seconds only words traverse its girth.'

The astonished captain here got up to walk.

'Our people live by millions in the cities ;

By nature they are homocentricous.

The rich man sometimes him with nothing
    pities,
If he himself is very ventricous.
And then we've ships,feet thick with iron for war,
And a smaller sort which, built for speed, goes
(At this the captain dropped his lower jaw)
Twenty miles an hour with her torpedoes.'

' Torpedoes !' said Oceanus.   ' What's that ?'

' The mightiest thing,' I answered, ' for a fight.
A torpedo no bigger than my hat
Would sink this ship, if filled with dynamite.'
Oceanus was very friendly now.
He came quite close and wondered who I was.
He made me now and then a gracious bow,
And said he'd like to know my name, because

If he should chance some day to steer that way

He'd pay a call and see these useful things.

' Well, what have you got more ? ' said Time ;

     ' come, say,

What you have told us keener interest brings.'

I told Oceanus my name, and said,

If he should drop his anchor near my shore

I'd do my best to see that he was fed,

And that he had enough to drink and more.

He grinned, and thought that after what he'd

     heard

Of things so wonderful in other ways,

That he would surely take me at my word,

And when he came he'd have some jolly

     days.

'We've seasons four on our revolving orb.

In spring the virtues of the earth are seen

To mount th' expanding stem, and thus absorb

The richness of the soil, whose vigorous green

Foretells abundance for the flocks and herds.

The second quarter sees great Helios grow

Less feeble in his rays, as on he girds

His gathering strength to shed a warmer glow.

Aurora in her golden summer time

Bids him good speed each morning as he drives

His blazing chariot in the year's full prime,

To ripen all our fruits and cheer our lives.

His journey travelled o'er the heaven's great arc,

His steeds with blood-red nostrils tint the west

With deepening flame, slow yielding to the dark

Of Erebus, the harbinger of rest.

The ripened corn and root crops laid in store,

Dianus holds his court for shorter hours ;

While rising Hesperus, scarce seen before,

Unfolds his light, the first of heaven's pale flowers.

The leaf now falls and active Nature rests.

Bleak winds and frosts hold undisputed sway.

Dismantled trees reveal vacated nests,

And winter sits enthroned amidst decay.'

'You've men of science and great learning too,'
Said Time.   .

         ' Indeed, we've many,' I replied
'From morn till night in search of something new.

It makes me think of home,' and then I sighed.
         .

' Don't be cast down,' said Time, ' you'll shortly
     see,

I hope, some sights that will your thoughts

    engage.

Where is the ship, Oceanus ?'

                        ' I'll see,'

He said, and rose with visage looking sage.

' Let's follow him,' said Time, 'and get some air,

My limbs are stiff with listening to you talk.'

A rolling ship and a precipitate stair

Made climbing needful, for I could not walk.

With some endeavour we were on the deck,

And found the sea was high with foaming waves ;

Of land I could not see a single speck ;

The furrowed ocean looked like new-made

    graves.

Time turned himself about and changed his face,

And seemed more grave and walked about alone.

This way and that he much increased his pace,

And now and then I thought I heard a groan.

Oceanus drew down the corners of his mouth,

And lifted up the hair that browed his eyes.

' Don't face the wind, but turn yourself to south !'

The captain loudly cried as out it flies.

' Ah, now I'm better, thank the stars for that ;

Your oily fish, Oceanus, was bad.'

The captain gave his abdomen a pat

And said, ' Oh no, the best that's to be had.'

' Well ! then, your wine was bad, there's some-

thing wrong,'

Said Time.   He felt ashamed to be like me.

I looked away and laughed both loud and long

At the dethronement of this deity.

So far Oceanus had not been told

Of Time's great project.   And so now he

    thought

He'd better tell before the vessel roll'd

Much worse.   Perchance, indeed, we might

    be caught

In some great storm ; who knows what Boreas

Might take it in his head some day to do.

Perhaps a stronger blow in store he has :

Great Æolus himself might say to you :

Since gentlemen you've placed your faith in me

Without arrangement for my being paid ;

I'll still my winds and make the calmest sea,

And where are you without Æolian aid ?

These thoughts sprung up and yielded in
    Time's mind

Some other thoughts that made him think it well

To broach his scheme, that they might better find

The heroine of the story he should tell.

Recovered from the shock he had received,

Time, with apologetic look, came up

To where we had amusedly perceived

The Avenger taste the mortal's bitter cup.

Time seemed to think, with us, that the design

Of human bowels was faulty, as regards

Their sailing qualities ; that some benign

God should haul in the slack superfluous yards.

Both Time and I were now in better trim ;

Less hot inside and cooler on the skin.

He eyed the captain and Oceanus eyed him,

As people do when neither can begin.

Time felt more steady and now stood erect.

Oceanus and I were looking out,

As people do who are trying to detect

Small objects on the water, when a shout

Stung our attention, and on looking round,

We saw the sailors rushing to the side.

Out of the water came a foreign sound,

From an unknown mouth that opened wide.

A sailor, better furnished than the rest

Inside his head, pushed through the eager throng

To shout a welcome to this novel guest.

A hawser overboard was trailed along

That he might take a hold and be hauled up.

Some sails are furled which makes the ship
sail slow.

He nearer comes and now has quite crawled up,

'Tis great Poseidon ; all are bowing low.

Oceanus and Time stepped from the crowd

And welcomed the great ruler of the seas.

Oceanus knew him well, and said aloud,

' A hearty welcome,' and then upon his knees

He seized his hand, and plunged it in his beard

To seal their friendship with a friendly kiss.

He walked back facing him, as if he feared

The consequences, should he act amiss.

Time stretched his limbs as far as they would
  reach,

As cocks and dogs do when a rival's seen ;

Like Ajax and Ulysses when they each

Descried the other and, with threatening mien

And stealthy pose, like panthers mad to eat,

Struck deadly blows to gain Achilles' shield

Poseidon and old Time did not so meet ;

Their contest left a much less bloody field.

Oceanus spread out his brawny arms,

The right towards Poseidon, the left towards
    Time,

Thus introducing them, with rarest charms

Of manner, which he thought were quite
    sublime.

Remaining each on his own chosen ground,

They both salute, erect and dignified.

The sailors open mouthed all stand around,

Discovering what each gesture signified.

Two gods on one deck is a grand occasion ;

So thought Oceanus, who showed that he

Would try, with courteous pressure and per-
    suasion,

To keep a while such august company.

A speechless period having been consumed,

All tried to find out what Poseidon's eye meant ;

We very naturally of course presumed

His mission was for something with his trident.

So far his Highness had not said a word ;

Amphibious creatures have not much to say.

Perhaps under water talking is not heard ;

The mouth at least can't open the same way.

Time thought Poseidon's visit somewhat strange,

And by his forehead showed he was perplexed.

He feared this incident might quite derange

The plans he had matured, and looked quite

      vexed.

At length Poseidon spoke.   He said that he

Had come to give a warning to the ship.

A tempest, bringing much calamity,

Had broken loose and soon would quite outstrip

The fleetest vessel urged by Æolian might.

' I warn Oceanus and give to him

Full time,' Poseidon said, ' before the night

Can lend still more confusion.'   Here his grim,

Storm-sculptured countenance looked black and

        drear,

And Time a little shrunk his massive form.

Oceanus looked round and thought he'd steer

For shelter from the fury of the storm.

The sailors stood aghast with awe and fear,

Feeling, as if in darkness, with their hands.

Then all approached until they were quite near

And stood around in eager little bands.

Time now was sorry that he had not told

Oceanus the object of this cruise.

If he had known he might have been so bold

As to communicate that piece of news.

Time made a hurried step and thought he'd speak

With Poseidon.   'Twas useless to delay.

How much is lost that might be gain'd by weak

Minds, courageless to speak what they should say.

Poseidon eyed the Avenger, and perceived

Some care had coiled itself about his brain ;

He thought he'd better wait and see relieved

This agitation, ere he spoke again.

At last Time's hesitation gathered strength

Enough to push the doubts from his mind's

    course,

And, binding effort's armour on, his length

To its full height he strained, and from its source

His boldest courage roused for this event.

As he approached, Oceanus and I

Made place for his antæan stride, which lent

To his appearance force and dignity.

Poseidon's trident with resounding clang

Employed the hollow ship to speak for him,

As o'er the deck its thundering accent rang,

And made her shake from keel to topmost rim.

Arrived at decent distance from the god,

Whose favour 'twas his object to secure,

He smiled and gave a friendly nod,

Which Poseidon returned with mien demure.

Oceanus gave orders to his men

That the two deities should not be pressed,

And they accordingly retired, and then

Time measuredly Poseidon thus addressed :

'O great Poseidon ! ruler of the sea ;

Creator and controller of the storm ;

Grant now your gracious aid to these and me,

And let your heart be moved with soft and warm

Affection towards the cause I shall disclose.

The potent voice of warning we have heard

Unseats our better sense ; and in us grows

Such feelings of alarm, that I no word

Can procreate sufficient to explain

The length and breadth and depth of the dismay

Which rests its weight on us.   Let not disdain

Coerce your kindly feelings ; that I pray.

Most noble Poseidon, whose boundless realm,

Your power and majesty so high enthrones,

Let your great genius direct the helm,

And steer our fortunes into peaceful zones.'

Poseidon let his countenance disclose

That Time had reached and somewhat touched

      his heart.

Yet in some lines 'twas seen (by him who knows

To read a face) doubt played a part.

Poseidon changed his attitude and said :

' Most noble ! puissant Time ; I must declare,

Surprise in me expands at your dread.

Why, surely ! potent Time commands the air ?

One single nod from your all powerful head,

I should have thought, could make the sea

> quite calm ?

The foulest weather would give place to fair,

If you decreed its forces should disarm.'

' Poseidon utters truth, I don't deny,

Regarding me ; but my first care must be

The good protection of this company.

'Tis that disturbs me, Poseidon.   Just see,

I pray, that your great chariot wheels be roll'd

From your Euboean palace in the sea,

And let your horses' hoofs and manes of gold
Stop this tempestuous calamity.'

' My horses and my chariot are not here ;
I was abroad, alone, when, sighting you,'
Poseidon said ; ' and then, I do much fear
It is too late to stay my fighting crew.
When once embarked, to rouse a stormy sea,
These demi-gods will not give in till they
Have drunk deep of the storm, and merrily
Their ravenous eyes full feasted on their prey.'

At this, Oceanus sprang up and cried,

' I'm sure he's going to drown the lot of us !'

He rushed away, with eyes distended wide,
Cursing Poseidon and his ποταμός.

Time thought 'twas best for them to go below,

And begged Poseidon for his company.

He called Oceanus and bade him show

The sea king down with fitting courtesy.

Some days had now run out, and we were far

Blown out to ocean by th' untiring wind.

The billows surged around, each bending spar

Its music in a chorus left behind.

The seamen so far had been well composed,

Nought fearing and nought caring, for they all,

Like sailors who engage themselves, supposed

Sometimes the blow would ripen to a squall.

But the coming of Poseidon made a change ;

For now the anxious men stand mouth to mouth,

In hot discussion as they interchange

A cataract of words.   Some looking south,

Some north, some west, some east, with

    tortured stare,

Pinch up their eyes' hard lids to point the sight,

And pierce the distance, and discover where

Poseidon's giant storm would take its flight.

While this disturbing scene went on above,

Time, down below, was using all his art,

Assisted by his new felt power of love,

To gain a corner in Poseidon's heart.

Oceanus was told at once that he

Had better go on deck and watch the sea.

To Poseidon it was no certainty

When it would come, or where it now might be.

The state saloon on board Time's worthy craft

Held him and Poseidon alone ; and they

Were seated talking, just abaft

The mizzen-mast, which stepped about mid way

In the saloon, gave them a rallying point—

As posts and pillars do wherever placed.

The Avenger fidgeted and worked each joint—

As people do who have no time to waste.

He used selected words to fit the ear

And find acceptance with the ocean king.

As he went on he warmed and came so near,

That Poseidon was rather wondering

What ailed his new - made friend, whose

    eagerness

Seemed urged along with some strong motive

    force.

In fact, he wondered at the meagreness

And importunity of his discourse.

' Now we are alone, Poseidon, let me say,

My being here is for a purpose set.

I'm on a voyage of great discovery,

And seriously your aid require.   Now let

Me for a moment have your friendly ear ;

The words I have to say are short and few.

Time's precious ; that I know.'

                ' And I much fear,'

Poseidon interposed, ' your stalwart crew

Must quickly make their good ship fit to war

Against the playful gambols of the seas

And travelling winds. So, say on good friend, for

We soon must stir and not sit here at ease.'

' Good !   Well, my story, long and short is this :

I'm looking for a wife.'

                ' A wife, indeed ! '

Poseidon said, and bulged his body out,

As male things do when thoughts of union breed

Desire in them and make its branches sprout.

' Yes,' Time said, much relieved; 'that is my wish,

And now, Poseidon, let me have your best

Endeavours to restrain this coming gale.

To you a storm is play ; but for the rest—'

Poseidon turned and cried, ' Take in all sail !'

Oceanus came running down the stairs,

And said, ' The air is thick with growing gloom ;

The waves are rising and right ill it fares

With those who are unprepared.'   A boom

Here swinging with the rising wind got loose,

And with a thundering crash smashed in the

poop.

Oceanus, unnerved, hurled his abuse

To right and left, till one excited group,

O'erwrought with mingled work and fear,

rushed aft,

Loud swearing, they would no more work the

ship.

Poseidon heard the oaths, at which he laughed,

And told Oceanus to use his whip.

The storm came on.   Poseidon told the crew

'Twas now too late to keep its fury down

And bade the captain try to heave her to.

The angry water seemed with rage to boil,

And spat with vicious energy its foam.

Each side and all around with strong recoil

The jealous waters seemed, as from their home,

To be intent upon the ejectment

Of this intruder.   Poised as for a breath,

On one still portion of the element

She hesitates, like some one nearing death.

But then, as if with gathered strength and
        weight,

Accorded to her by the angry sea,

She falls a prey in all her length, and straight

Into the yawning gulf, which seems to be

Designedly prepared, she plunges deep,

As if to mock at Fate by such a leap.

The friendly air embosomed 'tween her decks,

Now plays its part and gives a buoyancy,

Which out-manœuvres and completely checks

Æolian wrath, which would destroy and see

Apparently, straight sunder riven in twain

This noble craft.   Although the storm is young,

Its power unfolds with all its might and main,

As if from Time his purpose should be wrung.

Time and Poseidon now were on the scene.

The ocean king concerned to penetrate

And get his comprehension in between

The thoughts which Time had used to change

    his fate,

With eyes on the Avenger he declared,

That Reason had been strangled by his friend.

Poseidon wondered how he could have dared

To plan this expedition, and to send

So many people on so strange a cruise.

'Keep down your waters and you may depend,'

Said Time, 'it is to be!   If you refuse,

Perhaps it then will be!   And if my power

Extends to wielding sway o'er ocean's king,

What then will be your lot ?   Perhaps the hour

For your dethronement will be heard to ring

Throughout all seas and space.'

                                   Poseidon scowled,

And raised aloft his trident with a shout,

Which brought the Oceanides, who yelled and

        howled

And dived and plunged and rushed all round

        about.

' If Time dare war with me !' Poseidon said,

' Bring out your weapons and unloose your

        power ;

I'll wage, if you're determined to be wed,

Your path of love shall not be smooth one hour.

Great Æolus and all his satellites

Will join Poseidon, and their linkéd might,

Who never in their greatest battle fights

Have lost the day, will bring on you this

    night

Such fell destruction, as your darkest dreams

Ne'er pictured to Imagination's eye.'

Thus, with a crash that rove the deck in

    seams,

He dashed it down, and then again on high

He raised his trident, and with withering force

Swift dealt a blow, that sounded through the

    storm,

And vied with his own voice, which, gruffly

    hoarse,

Had lost with shouting all its tone and form.

Poseidon's angry threats resentment raised

In all the breasts of Time's devoted crew ;

Who one and all were silently amazed

At what Poseidon had the face to do.

Slow gathering round, Oceanus stood first,

They heard with wonder all he had to say.

He fearing, fortified himself and curst ;

In front the trident, he behind at bay.

'Such actions and such deeds,' in measured

      phrase

Spoke Time, 'are unbecoming such as you.

For gods to launch in such a wanton craze

Is poor example to my worthy crew.

What grave offence have they or I, my friend,

Advanced to Poseidon while here on board,

That he should in such fiendish fashion rend

Our good seaworthy deck, and thus afford

To us, who are a gentle, peaceful race,

Strong reason to resent such dastard deed ? '

The captain stooped as if he would embrace

And make this haughty bullying Hector bleed.

Oceanus and all the men looked fierce

And, as Time raised his hand, they one and all

Fell on Poseidon, who with deadly pierce

Drove through his trident, and with desperate

    fall

Fell men and god a tangled struggling heap.

Believing that the storm was born of him,

They seized and raised him, and with bounding

    leap

Capsized him in the sea. 'There let him swim!'

They cried, and shouting, rushed far up the ropes

To see the eruption of his fullest wrath.

The ship plunged on ; and down the steepest
    slopes
Poseidon with great fury and much froth
Pursued.   Meanwhile, he Pluto prayed and
    Zeus
To urge on Pluvius and the other powers,
That Time and ship and crew might to the
    deuse
Be quick transported.   Now for many hours
The storm had raged, and Time and all his men,
From captain to the smallest serf engaged,
Had had their fill of its great power, and then,
Through sharing in the sea fight they had waged,
Were weary and cast down with great fatigue.
Time prayed hard for some help from Æolus,
And ere the ship had run a further league
Against the storm, and right in front of us

There burst upon the whirling wind a light

Strange forked, and shooting like great tongues

> of fire.

Around by contrast looked like blackest night.

Poseidon close in front his chariot drove.

The gilded manes and hoofs, and gilded tire

Of his fleet wheels, as with high speed they rove

Deep furrows in the wave, were shining bright ;

And Poseidon himself, with fury filled,

First crossed and then recrossed the vessel's

> prow,

Designing her destruction ; for he willed

That Time should bend his knee to him, and

> now.

While prosecuting thus his fell intent,

Poseidon saw Time raise high both his arms

And gaze at that great light with wonderment.

The Ocean King, now harbouring alarms,

Bethought him Time was succoured by a friend.

The light enlarged, the fiery tongues spread out

And the great tempest slowly neared its end.

Time's crew were speechless, and they stared
    about

Dumbfounded at so marvellous a change ;

While Poseidon, whose anger was becalmed

At once by what he saw, kept out of range,

Not knowing how these comers might be armed.

With slow unfolding waves of whitest light

Came forth a maiden fair, of heavenly form,

Whose radiance shone against the outer night

Like brilliant lightning in the blackest storm.

Time clasped his hands and looked upon that
    face,

Around whose brow was writ *Eternity.*

Here Ambofilius came with quickened pace

And casting off his taciturnity

Spoke thus to him :

' Behold *there !* potent Time,

The saviour of our lives ! An angel fair

Stands on the heaven-lit clouds, a form

sublime,

Which fills my soul with rapture. I declare !

In Time's domain the fairest of the fair,

Whose every limb is perfect and complete,

Could not with this angelic form compare ;

So matchless pure, so gentle, and so sweet.'

So saying he stood still ; and all the rest,

Intent upon that apparition rare,

To see if it should further manifest

New wonders, motionless were standing there.

The storm was gone, and Erebus had drawn

In closer folds the mantle of the night.

Exiled Diana and Aurora's dawn

Now hand in hand restored the banished light.

The stately vessel and its element

In peace reposed, while baffled Poseidon,

Completely foiled in his abject intent,

Disturbs the calm as he retreats alone.

The golden gates of Phœbus are set wide,

And passing through the solar tide renews

The faded warmth, until at eventide

The ebb of Helios brings cooling dews.

Such strange emotions now awoke in Time

That he was lost entirely to himself

And stood on his toe-tips, as if to climb

The air and reach that heavenly angel elf.

Approaching slowly with extended hands

And head uplifted with transfixéd gaze,

He speechless wonders if she understands

That he's entranced and pleads that he may

    raise

Himself up there, where she in glory shrined

Implants in him a passion so profound,

That to aught else around his eyes are blind ;

Nor is his mind disturbed by touch or sound.

While looking thus he seemed to give a start,

As if a message from her gentle voice

Had breathed into the centre of his heart

And said, ' You are the lover of my choice.'

Then Æolus appears with jaded mien

Through efforts to control his struggling winds.

Eternity commands, and he is seen

Descending, as he cautiously unbinds

His element.   Approaching Time, he said :

' Most noble Time, my mission is to you.

Eternity requites your love and prays

That, if need be with some Æolian aid,

You for a time part from your noble crew

And join Eternity.'   He further said,—

' My potent element, at your command,

Is part unloosed, and ready to convey

Your puissant self, that you may claim the hand

Of the Eternal Queen.   I'll lead the way.'

Much agitation stirred the Avenger's breast,

So wondrous was the change that had been

      wrought

In his apparent destiny.   At best

His first endeavour would, he fully thought,

Bring nothing but despondency and grief ;

And even till within a short time since

He feared and entertained a strong belief

The vessel would be lost.   It might convince

Indeed, one wielding greater power than he,

That the designs of anger'd Poseidon,

To sink the ship beneath the raging sea

And leave Time battling with the storm alone,

Would end in harmony with his desire.

But, happily another fate was his.

A greater than Poseidon in his ire,

The fairest of great Heaven's deities

Had in the moment of their dire distress

Appeared in glory on the troubled scene,

Reducing Poseidon to nothingness.

She in unequalled splendour, Nature's Queen,

Like the most potent of all god-like powers,

Without a show of force apparent, wields

That subtle hidden strength before which

    cowers

The courage of the bravest, whose will yields

But to a ruthless foe omnipotent.

These thoughts, like quickened seeds in heated

    soil,

Responded to his sense of full content ;

Which, since the banishment of that turmoil

Whose flowering climax was Poseidon's rage,

Had to his mind restored some confidence.

His leading impulse now was to engage

His soul entire with all the incidents

Surrounding the changed course of his career.

He turned to Æolus and said, ' Good friend !

Pray lead the way ; ' and, with a mighty cheer

From those who thronged the ship from end to
    end,
Ascended slow with dignity and grace
Both Time and Æolus.   Upon that scene
Then fell a soundless calm.   Each eager face
Keen searching for what next was to be seen.
Slow rising, Time came near his new-found love;
But, as he came she calmly moved away,
And all the light around her and above
Seemed gently dying like a closing day.
Time followed, somewhat doubting in his mind
If what he saw was real or but a dream.
As distance grew 'twixt him and those behind,
His eyes watched closer the retreating beam
Which showed him where Eternity had gone.
At length it brightened, like a dew-decked
    flower,

Which rising Phœbus rests his rays upon

To gild it while it lives its little hour ;

And expanding slow, as children grow to men,

It widened to an avenue of light.

With long watching Time fell wondering, when

There visited his eye a new-born sight.

Just where the avenue of light begun,

A smiling fairy group stood clad in white

To welcome him.   More prominently one

Stood forth to offer welcome to the guest ;

With dimpled smiles and music in her voice,

She bade Time enter.   Then with all the rest

This captain of the band bade him make choice

Of many seats upon a radiant cloud,

Which, when he'd chosen, they pushed tenderly

With their sweet voices as they sung aloud.

The eyes of Time were much engaged to see

What unknown marvels might be here revealed.

He thought the mansions of Eternity

Would equal the great power which she could
wield.

As they sped on through endless change of
scene,

Nor tree nor flower came in his range of sight.

In all the boundless space was nothing green,

But shining crystal forms and warm pure light.

Some time had passed and his fair chaperones

Had filled his ears with choicest of their song,

When Time felt rather aching in his bones

And thought the way most lovely, but full long.

At this conjunction of two sets of thoughts,

Which seemed their seeds to sow in those
around,

Some new arrivals with their bright cohorts

Came up behind their pioneering sound.

Now rose the chorus of Time's body-guard

To mellowed harmony, a well-tuned choir,

Who joining those they met without retard,

Still grander chords are heard as they mount
        higher.

No trumpet sound nor blast with metal's ring

Swelled fuller that proud music which he heard ;

But all came from the throat, as angels sing,

Nor was there needed for support one single
        word.

Slow changing as a tribute stream whose hue

Scarce tints the parent flood with varying dye,

Around them crept, almost unseen it grew,

A light that changed the colours to the eye.

A perfect legion of attendants now

Gave Time their company. They looked on him

As something very strange, and wondered how

He came to look so very worn and grim.

Poor Time's experience on board the ship

Did not clean his dress, but rather soiled it.

He thought he'd better just delay the trip

While he performed the needful toilet.

So thinking, Time called forth his kindest smile

To tune the humour of his nearest friend ;

And as he asked the favour, all the while

His soul's sun shone its brightest to the end.

Perceiving quick the drift of his intent,

A talk ensued to find the best solutions,

Which caused no little burst of merriment ;

They never thought that Time required ablu-
tions.

His mission was a serious one ; he must,

He no doubt wisely thought, look quite his best,

And try and hide the centuries of rust

Which could not be concealed by coat and vest.

As we have said before, poor Time was bare,

At least in a sense ; there were some feathers

In his wings, but he'd not molted, and the hair

Showed contact with the stormiest of weathers.

In these great regions of Eternity

There were no signs of birth or of decay.

Time dwelt on this, and thought about
     paternity

With something of a feeling of dismay.

All that was there would there for ever be ;

What came, came perfect for Eternity.

There were no growing things, and he could see

No indications of maternity.

His feelings at these thoughts were rather
     harried ;

His countenance was twisted with some doubt.

'What is the use,' he said, 'of being married ?'

And then most eloquently looked about.

His fair companions seemed to understand

A little something of what troubled him,

Although they knew not that he sought the hand

Of their great Queen and peerless Seraphim.

However, being thus far on the road

'Twas useless turning back because of doubts.

A spot where he could wash himself they
    showed,

And he retired to where high water-spouts

Were ever growing like large crystal trees,

Whose spring and autumn-time, like twins
    together,

Saw leaves just born, yet dropping with the
    breeze,

Nor life nor death depending on the weather.

When well prepared, Time joined the company,

Who waited quite respectfully close by.

The expression of their faces showed that he

Now filled their eyes much more agreeably.

Before resuming his appointed place,

He interchanged ideas for a while,

To see if any were inclined to trace

From their remembrance the mode and style

Of living which Eternity maintained.

They yielded little to the questions put,

Which made him think they were much better

       brained

Then ordinary folks.   Then his right foot

He planted firm and filled his gaping seat,

When on they sped enveloped with new song,

Till all the ears were startled with a bleat

From one with better eyes, who saw among

The intermingled objects on before

The paradise Eternity enjoyed.

New vigour now incited all the corps,

Whose voices sounded pure and unalloyed.

Time raised himself as high as he could sit,

To close survey the objects coming near

And see Eternity's domain, if it

Resembled what he thought it would appear.

Small distant specks developed as they near'd

Into fresh hosts to form a new escort,

And the far-reaching outlines had a weird

And necromantic look, which gave, in short,

The mind of the spectator the idea

Some palace of unique design was there.

Dissolving slow, from indistinct to clear,

Now could be seen a shining lofty stair

With brilliant pillar'd arches just before.

Time's leading guide informed him it was there

Eternity received.   A massive door

Of sparkling crystal flanked with angel guards

Close fixed his eye, as nearer still they come.

Loud songs of welcome from the choicest bards

Thickened the air with undulating hum ;

And now and then a louder wave of sound

Tutors the ear part way to the intent

Of him who had composed.   Soon with a bound

The failing sense required, to show what's meant,

Dispelled confusion, and the gist was clear.

Far reaching, straight before and left and right,

Such scenes and sounds to ravish eye and ear

Time at his best had never known.   The sight

Now perfected in its details was such,

That his punctiliousness got out of joint ;

And some who watched him thought that he
was much

In danger of forgetting, that the point

Especially demanding his concern,

Was his reception by Eternity.

He thought of this on feeling his cheeks burn,

Remembering, no doubt, that he could learn

Particulars at leisure, by-and-by.

The crystal door now slowly opened wide,

And moving like a burning lava stream

There came a stately column, which Time eyed

As a waked sleeper stares fresh from a dream.

A staid ambassador moved at its head

Commissioned by Eternity to give

A hearty welcome to her guest.   He said,—

' Most generous, noble Time,—All who here live

Kneel at your feet and bid you be at home ;

Each one in your obedient servant's train

To the lowest.   And should you care to roam

Hereafter through Eternity's domain,

To paint upon your memory its sights,

'Twill be a joy if you their aid retain ;

The thought of it their choicest of delights.'

In presence of so reverend a sire

Time held himself with fitting dignity,

And with slow inclination (he was higher)

His head he bended low, that it might be

The measure of respect Time wished to
          show.

The ambassador saluted reverently,

And all behind, like waving corn, bent low

To pay due homage to Time's dignity.

'Good Sire!' said Time, 'you really honour me

Above what I could hope to have received ;

To be so kindly greeted, is to be

Of every embarrassment relieved.'

These courtesies exchanged they all retired,

Excepting just a few who stayed behind

To keep him company, for he required

In such a place some help to steer his mind.

This grand procession opened and there came

Another grander still, accompanied

By music that might very rightly claim

Perfection's warranty.   'Twas varièd

With such high skill and mathematic tune,

As if the harmony, like Nature's play

Upon the charmèd air, were deftly strewn

By some controlling superhuman sway.

Time stood surrounded by his first escort,

And either side large groups of his new friends.

The figure he had longed for had not caught

His eye, which searched the columns to their

      ends.

This one he thought must have her in its train,

And close he scrutinized with slow-drawn breath.

He looked until his eyes rebelled with pain :

' Does she repent ? ' he thought ; she lingereth.

A higher still exalted messenger,

With bearing of a yet more finished type

Made low obeisance to the Avenger,

As indication that their plans were ripe.

With courteous gesture and inviting phrase

He said, ' Eternity is now prepared

To give reception to her guest, and prays

That Time may further ceremonies be spared.'

So saying, he half turned him round, and showed

The way that Time should take.   With lifted

   hand

And finger pointed to the shortest road,

He smiled and moved, and Time and the whole

   band,

Like a tide breaking from its poisèd slack

And moving with unanimous consent,

Eternity's innumerable court marched back,

Preceded by the guest for whom they went.

The veritable climax now in reach,

With moments only between him and her,

Seemed to deprive Time of the power of speech,

And change the outline of his usual manner.

He bent with thought and then stood quite erect,

Wearing a smile as he would smile on her ;

Then pensive seemed as though he would elect

His best appearance, so that he might stir

And rouse Eternity to feel for him

No less than she professed when he was seen

In a more tragic light, which yet was dim,

And gave romantic features to the scene.

At length they reached the top of the long stairs,

And passed some distance through the crystal
     door

(A long procession when they walked in pairs),

Until all stood upon one crystal floor.

This was the lady's largest banquet-hall,

Where a repast in princely style was served ;

Each one took place until from wall to wall

The room was filled. Time felt somewhat
     unnerved

At such preparing, for he rightly thought

The whole of the arrangements were for him.

He wondered where from all these things were

    brought ;

Things that would satisfy the daintiest whim.

One mighty light shone from the ceiling top,

Whose rays all atoms pierced, however far,

And made each shine like one congealing drop,

A firmament with every speck a star.

In these exalted regions it appears

The human sense entirely has survived ;

They eat and drink, and, more than that, one

    hears

The girls are husbanded and the lovers wived.

Eternity, however, would not be

Endurable with babies cutting gums ;

' *Nous avons changez tout cela* ' entirely !

No multiplying there in little sums.

So with the other produce and the wine.

To have to plough and hoe and reap and grind,

And wash your clothes and hang them on the
line,

Is not employment of the highest kind.

The things required to tickle human sense

Were brought from somewhere—never mind
the place ;

Or whether they were paid in roubles, francs,
or pence,

Or whether, when they ate them, they said grace.

Such things with deities are not observed,

They only eat the kernels from the nuts.

They're cracked by unseen powers, and then
are served

By, as compared with them, mere Liliputs.

A fountain in the centre of the room

Yielded a sparkling wine in ceaseless flow,

Which spread upon the air a vinous bloom,

Reminding one of where the vine trees grow.

Cool crystal goblets stood in numbers round

The fountain's edge, inviting thirsty souls

To come and drink, and listen to the sound

Of splashing wines high foaming in the bowls.

A breathless stillness now reigned in the hall ;

Such quiet as there is in empty space.

Some waiting ended by a gentle fall

Upon the waveless air, which they could trace

As the beginning of a distant sound

Of many persons moving on the floor.

It slowly waxed in volume, and the ground

Made sympathetic movement, like the shore

Yields to the restless breakers in their race

To gain the finite limit of the sea.

A herald now comes on with quicker pace

To tell the coming of Eternity,

And as he speaks the sound of treading feet

Wells up between the buzz of busy talk.

Time gave a start, as though he meant to meet

His love, and fondly greet her while they walk.

He hesitates.   The herald nearing where

Time had by invitation fixed his place,

Persuaded him politely to repair

To a position where his noble face

Could by the whole assembly best be seen.

A lofty opening in one wall contained

Eternity's bright throne, where she, as queen,

Held her great court and always entertained.

On one side was another throne designed,

Which had a look of newness in its build.

The sculptured crystal round it brightly shined;

But no one yet its ample seat had filled.

Time took a place beside the second throne

And watched the grand procession filing by.

At last Eternity appear'd; she walked alone.

Time warmed from head to foot. Her smiling eye

And perfect beauty grasped his every sense;

And as one link holds fast the prisoner chained,

So beauty's link in strength was so intense

His eyes were chained; yet, he his best
    refrained

From showing to the company around,

How deep that face had wrought upon his soul

Its mark indelible. Indeed, he found,

On searching through and through the endless
    roll

Of his experience, there was no sign,

Which centuries between could not erase,

That he had felt an impress so divine

On his whole being.   So sat Amaze

Full pictured in the countenance of Time.

Eternity on her side, Time on his,

Made courteous recognition, as the prime

Introduction to all ceremonies.

Her chief attendants aided her to rise

And take her place upon the centre throne;

While others, pointing with their smiling eyes,

Invited Time, who raised himself alone.

Thus, this august assembly was complete,

And that locked silence which so far had ruled,

Yielded its unseen bars to strains of sweet

Refreshing harmony, which soothed and cooled

The warm excitement caused by this event.

The feast was served, the foaming wine imbibed;

The lover's cup went round, the air was rent

With merriment which cannot be described.

The singers who sung first with their instructor

Sung well in tune when they had had no wine ;

Bacchus perhaps is not a good conductor

Inoculated fresh from his best vine.

At length, as on the planets down below,

An exodus to cooler air took place.

In twos and twos where lights were burning low

They wandered ; touching sometimes face with

    face.

The banquet hall being empty, saving two,

Time felt, presumably as lovers do

When they perceive the time has come to woo,

He must begin ; but how he scarcely knew.

In his position he must not be shy,

Supposing he felt modest ; so he rose

And in a gentle voice and tenderly,

But with some confidence as one who knows

His suit is part accepted, he then said,—

‘ Eternity ! my power of speech is gone.

Like a frail flower whose tender bloom is shed

By the sun's scorching heat, that falls upon

And unopposéd steals its feeble life,

The flower of my poor speech before the gaze

Of your refulgent beauty, shuns the strife

And sinks to impotence before its withering

      rays.'

Then clasping close his hands upon his breast

And leaning forward with slight bended head,

He seemed to lose the power to say the rest ;

But, gaining courage, he revived and said,—

‘ Eternity ! I would that I could say—

What in me lies.   It is an endless train

Of nourished hopes and fears, that on me prey :

Hopes, like the new-born flowers in summer rain,

Full blooming even now, yet of frail life,

Until you ratify your plighted love.

Eternity! say you will be my wife?'

So saying, he moved nearer to her throne

And watched her eyes, whose glances fixed
    above,

Seemed searching for a reason to postpone

Responding to Time's vehement appeal.

Becoming modesty her manner clothed,

Which strengthened his desire, and made him
    feel

He could not rest until they were betrothed.

She spoke not, but he saw her tender frame

Like chords of music when the sound steals
    forth.

Emotion in her trembled like a flame,

Which made him rise, and his right hand hold

forth,

Exclaiming in high key, yet dulcet tones,

' Celestial angel ! say you will be mine ? '

Her hand responded, and in semi-tones

Of that peculiar sweetness feminine,

Which gives to life a thrill of exquisite

Sensation, worth a thousand years without,

(By which Time's nature, oh ! so like is it

In all, was by Eternity drawn out),

The music of her heart awoke his ear

And banished from his soul its chill reserve ;

Dismissed for ever all his doubt and fear

And gave him her for ay to love and serve.

Eternity stepped gently from her throne

And on her lips received a lingering seal

To this great compact.

'Never more alone!'

Time loud exclaimed. 'My life will now be real,'

So saying, he looked down and smiled on her

A smile born of the fullest happiness,

Which would on him for evermore confer

The highest of delights and blissfulness.

This episode well ended, both walked out

And weaved their voices in between the rest

Of those which bloomed with melody and song.

The eyes of some who met them showed they

     guessed

That love's sweet drama was not very long.

The closer friends Eternity retained

Read, in the two being joined, what had occurred,

And came with feelings warm and unrestrained

To wish her every joy. The news so stirred

The sentiments of all in her domain,

That ere great Time and she had wandered far,

Great cheering rose, and rose, and rose again,

Until the air, with the repeated jar

Of cheer defeating cheer, was so upheaved,

That like Poseidon and Æolian fight,

Which worked the ocean into black and white,

It shook and trembled like a damsel grieved

By some deep lover's sorrow unrelieved.

Before the shouts had spent their utmost sound

The other lovers' sighs were no more breathed ;

But an immense excited throng came round

And with their lifted wings Time's forehead
         wreathed.

Her fondest friends Eternity upraised

And singing bore her to ethereal heights.

Time would not leave her. He still fondly gazed,

And spreading too his ample wings, the flights

They flew he followed, until coming near

The banquet-hall, where fresh repasts were

    spread,

They both descended midst a mighty cheer

Of welcome, tears of fullest joy being shed.

The temper of the banqueters had changed ;

Nor Time nor his beloved were they the same.

The Avenger was himself and not estranged

As when he came. He called his love by name,

And said it in a way that showed so well

That his poor heart had found a resting place.

He seemed to speak with all and try to tell

How happy now he was ; how he'd found grace.

The thrones were empty, and they sat among

The merry revellers who drank their health ;

Time stood the centre of a lively throng

Inflated by his new acquired wealth.

' My worthy friends,' he said, ' I will propose

A toast, the proudest of my lengthened life.'

He raised his bowl on high, while pressing close,

They flocked around him and his future wife.

The company entire, like autumn winds

Stripping their vestments from the shivering trees,

Rose like an angry storm, whose power unwinds

And grows into a gale by quick degrees.

A thousand tankards sprang above their heads,

To float upon a sea of wine-born cheers,

Which ript the air and seemed to leave in shreds

The mouths that shouted, till the eyes dropt tears.

Songs to Anchises and winged Eros filled

The wine-clad air with joyous strains of mirth.

Eternity passed here and there, and many
     spilled

What they would drink, in trying to give birth

To long word compliments in praise of her.

The male surroundings of her graceful court

Sang bacchanalian songs, and tried to stir

Time's nature till it was so deeply wrought

And moved to its profoundest depths, that he,

In stentor tones, raised up his time-worn voice

And made the banquet-hall with melody

Resound.   These songs of revelry so choice

At length wore out entire their origins,

And one and all exhausted sobered down.

Time seeing this, and that the hairy chins

Of older men, with wider spread renown,

Were shelved upon their hands to rest the head,

He parleyed with Eternity and said,—

' My noble friends !   Eternity commands

Me to stand forth and unreserved declare

Her deepest gratitude.   At your kind hands

We have received attention, we both share,

So far surpassing our highest thought,

That for Eternity and me I say

We are truly grateful.   'Those who brought

Me with such care along the charming way,

Which leads direct to this enchanted spot,

Will feel, I hope, that what I do not say

E'en measures more my gratitude than what

My poor untutored eloquence declares.'

With this, Time spread his hands and thanked

       them all,

And the assembly, as they came, in pairs

Filed out, leaving two only in the hall.

Eternity and Time, now better known

Each to the other ; she like a creeper

Made her beginnings, as she might have grown

Had she been ivy, and he her keeper

The solid oak.   She laid her slender arms

In leaning loveliness and on him pressed.

He, warm reception gave her matchless charms

And kissed her, fondly pillowed on his breast.

Two halves of Nature seeking long to meet

Each in the other, like Phœbus in the flower

Of some fair rose, by touching kindled heat

And gave to life its highest, fiercest power.

Her eyes and his in one sensation mixed,

And for a moment they were lost in sense ;

She, as the ivy round the oak, was fixed

In his herculean yet loving arms, whence

A disentanglement no favour found

In him or her.   At length, like Nature's rose

Whose leaves are falling on the parent ground,

Their love had partly bloomed. The deepest
    throes
Of love's immeasurable heav'nly bliss
Were yet unfathom'd, and to her unknown.
The bloom was only gone, the virgin kiss ;
Love's flower was in the bud, not yet full grown.
Time sighed and fondly looked on her again,—
' My darling angel! we must part a while,'
Said he, and rising with a gentle strain
He raised her hand and kissed it with a smile.

' Eternity ! the laws of heaven demand,
That man and woman must submit to be,
According to the laws of every land,
Together joined with fitting ceremony :
We must be married. I will to my home
With my good friends who wait in yonder ship.

Stay here a while, sweet love, and while you

    roam

In this divine domain, I'll make my trip,

And have prepared a vast and splendid show,

Of which the head shall be my angel queen ;

A *marriage*-show Eternity ! We'll go

Through 'space infinite. Never has there been

Of all the pageants since creation dawned

Procession like to this I shall prepare ! '

Again he fondled her and softly fawned

Upon her, smoothing with his hand her hair.

' Good Time, my life is changed,' she said, and

    sighed ;

' Your coming has brought something dear to me.'

Her tender feelings melted and she cried,

And looked upon him with simplicity.

'The time we are parted, love, will be so brief,'

He said, in a half plaintive, whining tone ;

'While I am gone my life will all be grief.

My heart will feed on hope while I'm alone,

When sweet Diana comes in her white gown

To bid Dame Chaos raise her dusky veil,

I'll wake, and bid her weave a lovely crown

Of Phœbus' choicest rays, and I'll not fail,

My pretty queen, to have it in due time

To sit enthroned upon your maiden brow,

To throw before its gleam, when we shall climb

The gilded heights of heaven, a shining prow

To our great marriage train. Now we must part.

Eternity, call out your noble court

And let me say adieu before I start.

They are so kind, your friends ; I feel, in short,

As if I'd lived here many joyful years.

I've been so happy these few merry days,

And now as the dread hour for parting nears

My soul burns dim ; in mourning are its rays.'

' Dear Time,' she said, ' what is to be, must be,'

And, calling her attendant, bade her tell

The members of her court to come and see

Time go, and take affectionate farewell.

Eternity's great suite spread o'er the plain,

And Time's escort, who brought him to his love,

Made ready to escort him back again.

His chariot cloud descended from above,

And he in his best language thanked them all.

' My friends,' he said, ' my noble sires and
      dames !

It's usual when one can use you all,

And be familiar with your Christian names,

To say good-bye and take a friendly leave

Before I go and part from you a while.

I do not hide from you how much I grieve.

My heart is sad, and yet it is futile

To water useless thoughts with wasted tears,

And grieve o'er pleasures that have run to seed.

To sow enjoyment's seed to me appears

Rather a wiser toil.   Our time, indeed,

Is always better spent in looking straight

Into the future, where our life to come

Must be ploughed up and sown ; e'en then our
     fate

Will much depend on how we reap.   Welcome !

You said to me so kindly when I came ;

To you, my friends, I bid a fond farewell.

Eternity now soon will take my name.'

At this there rose a shout and frantic yell

Of endless cheers, which rent the startled air.

Repeated oft, and gathering greater strength,

Such joyous sounds before were never there.

Throughout the breadth of her domain and

      length

Ran messengers to tell the happy news ;

And 'mid excitement never more intense

All honor'd them with compliments profuse.

' At last,' said Time, ' my friends, farewell !   I

      hence,

Indeed, must go.   Eternity, good-bye

Once more, good-bye.   A little while, my love ;

Only a little while, *Eternity !* '

The loving fingers parted, and above

His chariot cloud sailed steadily away.

K

The music of sweet voices filled the air,

And as his eyes looked fondly on the grey

Cold mist that shrined his love, he thought of
　　their

Great happiness which he should now prepare.

The gentle elves who formed Time's charming
　　suite

Were all well known to him, and seemed to
　　share

In his delight, and think it quite a treat

To follow in his train, and see him safe

Returned on board among his waiting crew;

Who must, Time thought, have now begun to
　　chafe,

And like all other wights want something new.

So on they sped, until at length they reach

The same old spot where they all met before.

Time's gratitude o'erflowed.   He hoped that
    each
Would join Eternity, when to his shore
She came.   'Farewell, my friends,' he said,
    ' good-bye ! '
And disappeared with rapid downward flight,
As from a mountain's summit in the sky
An eagle races with the morning light.
His soul renewed, his whole vitality
Responded to his newborn joy in life,
As those must feel who immortality
Receive to compensate for deadly strife
And years of pain and trouble here below.
Descending from the paradise on high,
Time soon perceived the restless, shifting glow
Which moving waters picture from the sky.
No ship was seen, no crew, no signs of life :

Time traversed leagues and leagues, 'twas all
    the same.
He thought with anguish of his future wife,
And trembled like a reed throughout his frame.
' Oceanus !' he called, but called in vain.
The waters answered not, nor sight nor sound.
He strained his eyes till straining gave them
    pain,
Until he feared he surely must be drown'd.
Time's power was great, but not so great that he
Omnipotent could be.   Where was his crew ?
Poseidon had perhaps enraged the sea
And clean destroyed them all, because he knew
Time would return and might their aid require.
These thoughts ran through his agitated mind
When something caught his eye.   A speck of
    fire

Seen far away ; the lantern of some kind

And succouring friend perhaps in search of him.

It grew and multiplied full many times,

And like a comet swiftly seemed to skim

Across the sea.　Like iron on flint, sometimes

It struck a shower of sparks, which lighted far

The water and the heavens with glowing fire.

It hurried on ; it was a golden car ;

He saw Poseidon and the golden tyre,

And mane and hoof that he had seen before.

He looked enraged as if he did pursue

Some enemy he hotly hated and would kill.

As he approached the power he wielded grew ;

The trident grew, and seemed Time's mind to fill

With some suspicion that Poseidon meant

To take revenge.　Time now perceived his eye

Fixed straight on him.　He saw his full intent

And raised himself while Poseidon rushed by.

' The curséd of all curséd on this sea ! '

Cried Poseidon, with features puffed with ire,

And rein'd his chariot round that he might see

Where Time had flown.   The burning brilliant
    fire

Which Poseidon created with his speed

Half blinded him.   Time was, however, there,

And calmly waited, taking little heed

Of this great burst of anger, till the glare

Of light had disappeared.   At length he spoke,

And asked Poseidon if he'd seen the ship.

Poseidon heaved with rage as if he'd choke.

He curs'd and swore and bit his under lip,

And challenged the Avenger to a fight.

' Your ship is smashed,' he said; ' your crew are
    drowned,

And I will have revenge! It is my right!'

Time hearing this flew gently round and round,

And watching seized a portion of the car.

Poseidon raised his trident for a blow

But missed his aim. So heavy was the jar

That he upset himself, when Time let go,

And seizing Poseidon well round the waist

A deadly struggle brought out all their strength.

The chariot moved; the horses in their haste

To gather speed fell their full sprawling length

Upon the boiling sea. Both fiercely tugged,

Urged by Poseidon to drag on the car.

With biting grip the deities both hugged;

They seemed to be about upon a par.

Poseidon wrenched and pulled and dragged and tore,

And slashed his trident in the surging sea.

The more Time pinched, the more Poseidon
swore.

'Tell where my ship is, and I'll let you be,'
Said Time, as well as he could speak between
Spasmodic efforts to take in the air.

'Let go!' Poseidon howled. 'You hurt my
spleen!'
And turning quick he seized Time by the hair.

'Let go! you villain!' Time roared in his turn,
And shook Poseidon till he could not speak.
Their blood waxed hotter, and each tried to spurn
With all his might the other, when a leak
Sprang in the car, and both these heroes stood
Waste deep in water fighting to the death.

Poseidon kicked and slashed, and thought he
    should
Make Time give in at last for want of breath ;
But the Avenger held his ocean king
With such uncompromising, steady grip,
His arms around him like an iron ring
The more he kicked were less inclined to slip.
At last Time spoke inside his angry soul,
Stirred by fears of a coming tragic end,
And muttered with a gruff and rumbling roll
A thick set oath that he would shortly rend
In shivering shreds this monster of the deep.
' Wilt cease thy throbbing throes !' Time yelled.

' NO !' roared Poseidon, as with raving leap
He made a frantic effort ; but Time held
Him with such fixed and unrelaxing clutch

That like two trees as saplings inter-grown

They quivering stood. Said Time, ' By Jove !
     Is such

This devil's damnable design !   I own

If his intent is loss of him or me,

Then my past centuries of spended power

And all the flower of my best energy

Shall be revived and centred in this hour.'

So saying, with gigantic heave he tore

Poseidon from his grip upon the car,

And hurled him howling on the chariot floor.

' Hell's flame-points paint with rankling, fester-
     ing scar

Your curséd ugliness,' said Time, who seized

The heated trident of his humbled foe,

And smashed it with one blow, and thus appeas'd

His deep volcanic wrath.   Time then, with slow
Close-watching look, the crushed Poseidon ey'd,
Who panting lay with scowling, fiendish stare,
And might for aught the other cared have
     died.
The mast-high bright and piercing flare
Which Poseidon's great car stirred in the sea
Fell on the eyeballs of Oceanus,
Who had for days with great anxiety
The ocean searched.   Directions various
He had pursued without or rest or sleep.
Time saw the ship as it was changing tack.
The brilliant glare reflected from the deep
Fell on the spreading sails, which threw it back.
Time raised himself and gave a mighty shout,
When Poseidon rose too ; but he was done.
If not before, his master he'd found out.

He'd fought with Time, and Time the fight
    had won.
Each kept a watch upon the other's eye,
The index of the living thoughts within.
Time told Oceanus to keep the ship close by,
And have his quarters fit to take him in.

'Now, then, Poseidon, shall we part as friends
Or foes ?   I am of those who are fond of peace ;
But, Time's determination never bends
Where there's injustice.   Let ill-feeling cease.'

Poseidon drew the anger from his face
And loosed the floes of rage which Time had
    froze
Around his shrunken soul.   His earn'd disgrace
Weighed heavily, like grief on one who knows

The weight is wages for the work he's done ;

But Justice made her voice heard in his heart.

'We've fought,' said Poseidon, 'and you have

    won :

I know it was my fault.   Before we part

I beg you, puissant Time and all your crew,

To wash your memories in this virgin sea ;

Forget the past.   Let not the minds of you

And your brave comrades think the worse

    of me

For letting my strong nature rule my will.'

Then each the other's hand with friendly grasp

Enclosed, while all the ship's crew, standing still,

Close watched till each relaxed his tightened

    clasp.

'Farewell,' said Time, 'I hope when next we
    meet
Each may the other serve with friendly aid.'

Poseidon bowed and Time made his retreat,
Full satisfied to seek the cooler shade
On board his ship.   The unfurled sails out-
    spread
And forward on her path the ship proceeds ;
Poseidon baled his car and drove ahead,
Thus ending peacefully these tragic deeds.
Oceanus and Ambofilius came,
The sailors also, open-mouth'd and ey'd,
Surrounded Time and whispered loud his
    name.
'Where has Time been!' they then with
    wonder cried.

'We all have feared that Time had been de-
stroyed,'
Oceanus exclaimed, as he embraced
The proffered hand Time gave him, everjoyed
To find what he had searched for in such
haste.
Then Time narrated all he'd done and seen.
He spoke of all the wonders there on high.

He said, ' My friends, one day you'll see my
queen ;
You'll see my bride, my wife, Eternity ! '

At mention of this name his figure shook.
The crew all raised their arms and cheered and
cheered,
Moved to the demonstration by his pleaséd look.

Time asked Oceanus where now he steered.

'Put the ship straight for home, my worthy friend,'

Said Time.   'Spread out at once your largest

    sails

And let this voyage quickly near its end.

The work I shall administer entails

The funding of much thought, and measurement

Of divers things momentous to my plans.

I hope good Ambofilius is content ?'

Said Time, as he embraced and shook his hands.

I said, 'Indeed, we've had an anxious time.'

Within myself I did not feel content,

And thought in fact 'twas something like a

    crime

That he should leave me when to Heaven he

    went.

When asked about these things, I plainly told

His majesty I did not like the way

He had retired and left me in the cold.

I wished to hear what he had got to say.

' Good Ambofilius, come with me below ;

I much regret the tedious time you've had.

I must confess, when I was called to go

With Æolus, I was so nearly mad

And smitten with a frenzy of delight

That, like a startled wave upon the shore,

Or a bright star that's quenchéd in the night,

My memory simply died, and I no more

Held in my head the reins, but of one sense.

That sense, good Ambofilius, you know well ;

To me it was a stranger then ; not now !

My worthy friend, there is no parallel

Throughout the regions where Inheritance

Has given to all the senses power to grow,

Between that one of love and any other.

It is a flame no power in heaven can smother.'

' I saw the flame burn bright, good Time, in you.

Your face was radiant when that form appeared ;

And as one saw her with a clearer view,

The hearts of all on board were lost.   I feared,

Indeed, I might myself have lost all sense,

So bright and lovely was that angel face.'

Time smiled, and said, ' I had full recompense

In visiting her heavenly dwelling-place.'

The ship sailed on and we were straightway
bound

For Time's domain, when one fine sunny morn

Oceanus asked Time what he had found,

Thus manifesting that desire inborn

Which marks the race.   The ship's crew
    gathered round,

And Time, the greatest hero they had known,

By virtue of his latest great exploit,

Seemed to stand higher, as if he felt he'd
    grown

In stature since his clever and adroit

Ascent to heaven, and subsequent defeat

Of one whom all admired for his prowess.

' My worthy friends,' said Time, ' I will repeat

Of what I saw, some things.   You cannot guess,

Nor could the finest poet's finest lines

Portray the perfect splendour of the scenes.

When coming near the point of heaven's

    confines,

A tempered frame of clouds the beauty screens.

I near the hallowed entrance filled with fear,

Tho' all seemed peaceful in its glory there.

As I approached the fairy forms appear

Of angels floating in the buoyant air.

Perceiving me, the sounds of perfect song

Unfold their balanced parts and fill the ear

With such enthralling, captivating, strong,

And sense-encharming coil, that, save a tear

Which burst from my enraptured spell-bound

    soul,

I was entranced.'

               ' So wonderful, good sire !'

Oceanus remarked ; ' pray, do proceed,

And tell us all you saw; we beg the whole,

If you will satisfy a keen desire

Which animates us all on board, indeed!'

So hearing, with pursed mouth and knitted brow,

Time leaned his massive form against the mast,

And thus related at his leisure how

He reached Eternity's domain at last.

'My worthy friends,' said Time, 'you saw me
    leave.

The noble Æolus gave friendly aid,

And I must tell you that I sadly grieve

(For fighting does all fighters much degrade)

For my encounters with Poseidon's might.

We gave no cause of quarrel; that you know.

'Twas he begun! 'Twas he desired the fight!

He fought; and when you came was glad to go.'

At this a thundering cheer went up aloft,

And eyes on eyes with satisfaction fed.

Time smiled with much delight also and coughed

To clear his throat for what he had not said.

' I said before, the music there was grand.

You've seen, my friends, great Helios in full burn,

When he looks straight at you; but you can't
    stand,

And with your little eyes outstare his stern,

Creating, penetrating, warming light ?

From your imaginations sweep the dust

And picture Erebos's darkest night.

Think further, and remove the gather'd rust

Which your dull life gives your intelligence.

Think of the brightest moon that sits the
    heavens,

With ten times brighter glow, yet with intense,

Not overpowering warmth and light, which

    leavens

The heat and power that Helios might dispense

If he had reached full age and strength and light.

Those regions up above seem never cold.

I saw no rain ; I felt no chilly night ;

I saw no painéd young, no suffering old.

The life up there seemed full of joy and mirth.

I saw them always laughing ; not a cry

Of heart-sore weeping ever found its birth

In that fair land, where no one lives to die.

The morning and the evening seemed to be

Like man and wife below, conjoined in one.

A measured warmth, with light enough to see,

Accompanied the evening as the morning had

    begun.

A friendly feeling reigned, no enemies

Made discord ; but the harmony maintained

Bloomed in perennial amenities,

Like sweetest perfume for all time sustained.

The road we traversed when I first set out

. Was like a picture, where all things are made

   made

Of choicest form and kind.　I looked about

But saw no traces in the deepest shade

Of dawning death or lingering decay.

All things looked bright and fresh and clean

   and new.

Equality in life as in the endless day,

Expelled degrees, to make each one of you,

When your turn comes, as high in heaven's

   domain

As the imperial Cæsar of the sphere

In which my friend hopes to enjoy again

The pleasures he does not discover here.'

Time looked at Ambofilius as he spoke,

And their eyes held a converse dress'd with smiles.

Time's friend remembered well when he awoke

And found himself in his great hall erewhiles.

I said, ' I hope, good sire, as time goes on,

The same kind friend who brought me to your

      hall,

Whoever is the estimable person,

Will not forget that he is bound to call

And rid you of your guest in proper time.'

' Fear not, my friend,' said Time, ' rest well

      assured

That when you've had enough of this dull clime,

You'll be reclaimed and not at all injured.'

With this Time then resumed his narrative.

' We passed through lands of crystal purity ;

The eye deep revelled in the changing scene.

All things enjoyed a fixed maturity,

As if from the beginning they had been

Perfection finished for all time to last.

The angel elves who charmed me by the way

Were fashioned like to you ; but each was cast

In such a perfect mould, in such refined array,

That the delighted eye grew dim to see

Such matchless beauty in society.

My friends, you weary with the things I tell ? '

A rustling of desire ran through the crowd

As Time said this.   His words were like a spell.

He saw it, and felt naturally proud.

The theme to him was like the sun in heaven,

It warmed, it cheered, it gave his soul a life,

Which nothing else in his career had given.

He raised his hands sometimes and said, ' My

      wife ! '

In accents which like thunder spoke within ;

But not a sound came from his love-sick breast.

He thus discoursed and would again begin,

When one man cried, and then cried all the rest,

' The land ! The land ! Our native shore again ! '

The scene now changed, the gathering dispersed.

All order disappeared, none could restrain

Their eagerness to disembark the first.

All crowded in the ship's capacious bows

To gaze upon the throng that lined the shore.

They knew Time's coming home would surely
    rouse
Greater enthusiasm than they had seen before.
Oceanus his orders loudly roared,
To get attention from his underlings.
He knew full well that such a scene aboard
Is what so often some big blunder brings.
I thought, I am coming back to this bright spot,
But what my future is I've no idea ;
'Twas useless asking Time if he knew what
Was to become of me.   He'd say, my dear,
Have patience and enjoy your little hour,
The future will reveal what is your fate.
I should reply, my dear, if I'd the power,
I should prefer at once to emigrate.
These gorgeous paradises don't suit me ;
I feel acutely my position here.

If this is what they call equality,

I'd rather in my world be made a peer.

The sight along the shore was very grand ;

Time's suite entire had come to welcome him.

Some stood, some sat upon the sand,

And others waded out who could not swim.

The sailors signalled with their lifted hands,

And like a cluster of dressed summer trees

The captain hung his masts with flags and
      bands

Of tapering streamers, which by small degrees

Waved into nothing, like the green ribb'd sea

As distance makes each wave a smaller size.

Time overjoyed that he successfully

Had found a wife, cast up his grateful eyes

As if he looked upon a higher power,

Expressing many thanks for his success.

He came upon the shore ; it was the hour

Of full mid-day.   Great Helios in his dress,

A million miles of flame, sent fiery darts

O'er corruscating sea and glittering sand,

And each of Time's great retinue upstarts

At his approach ; the nearest kissed his hand.

All circled round him in a surging mass

Like water whirling in a punctured pool.

They came so close the Avenger could not pa ss,

And felt the opposite of very cool.

Time told Oceanus to come on shore

And let his people follow close behind.

He went with Ambofilius on before,

And as they walk and talk and gently wind

About and through up hill and down the dale,

Time said, 'My friend, I must now quick prepare,

And you must help me, for I cannot fail

To have all things arranged in such a rare

And perfect style as never in this land

Was seen before.   I shall call up the gods

And ask the greatest powers that be, to band

Together for my show, and I'll lay odds

The marriage of Eternity with me

Shall bring more eyes in line than an eclipse,

When Luna and great Helios chance to be

So near that he can snatch with his thick lips

A passing kiss.'   So saying he turned round

And halted on the summit of a hill.

' Good Ambofilius, you know this ground ? '

' Indeed, I do,' I said ; 'its beauties still

Hold me entranced as when I saw them first.'

Time said, ' Send on my people ; let them go

Before into my halls and slake their thirst,

While I from here prepare for my great show

By calling on the gods.   Stand by my side.'

Then with majestic mien and stately pose,

With head erect and mantled in his pride,

One hand he hipped, the other up he throws,

And speaking with a voice tuned by his love,

He calls upon his brother gods above.

' Up, Boreas ! distend your northern ears !

Blow out the trumpets of your frigid zone

And wake creation ; for 'tis many years,

I'll wager, since you heard, and you will own,

When you have heard it in befitting rhyme,

'Tis strange what I shall tell.   Wake ! Boreas,

     wake !

And gather for this once from every clime

Your sleeping winds, and let them for my sake

Pay homage, for 'tis I who call, old Time.

Send out your messengers to east and south,

Tell west to blow and ope' your northern mouth.

Let circling storms bear on their wingéd wings

The joyful news, that all may join my suite.'

' What is the joyful news that good Time

      brings ? '

Said Boreas, as he lighted on his feet.

' The news, my worthy friend ! just hearken you.

I've been to heaven ! the glorious paradise ;

I've had real angels in my retinue ;

I've seen, my worthy friend, with my own eyes

Such wonders, Boreas, as to you or me

M

Are wonders of perfection's perfect type.

I took my friends and sailed across the sea

To find a wife.   My plans are nearly ripe

To bring my marriage to the joyful end.'

' A wife !' said Boreas; 'Have you found a wife ?'

'Ay! have I !' cried he, with an upward bend

Of his eyebrows, which showed his lengthened
  life

Had gained in strength since he was last at
  home,

Which made him think 'twas good sometimes to
  roam.

' I want the gods of our fraternity

To lend their presence to adorn my suite.

My love, the sweet, the pure Eternity,

Will journey to a spot where we shall meet.

Now, Boreas,' said Time, ' will you assist,

And ask the brother gods to my great feast ?

Don't take refusal ; mind, you must insist

That all, the most exalted and the least,

Do me this honour.   Now, Boreas, hear

What further I shall say.   The gods must come.

Then next the goddesses must all appear.

You should bid Jupiter a good welcome ;

Ask Mars and Bacchus, Mercury and Sol.

My friend Poseidon, and the low Hades

For this event perhaps you may enrol,

Together with Hephaestus, if you please.

Eternity, I'm sure, will Venus choose

For her surpassing loveliness and grace ;

At least, 'tis my belief; for he who woos

Values perhaps the most a pretty face.

Another queenly consort is Juno.

Her rank among the goddesses is high ;

She's female Jupiter in heaven, you know,

And keeps her sex in order generally.

Give these a call good Boreas ; let each

Hear from you, polished phrase in copious

　　　showers,

In your best colours, like a painted speech.

Bid them all come in language's best flowers.

Aurora and Diana should come next ;

We must of course have these to light the way.

If they are not first, I hope they'll not be vexed ;

Not being in front will not affect their ray.

Then for domestic comfort we should take

The gentle Hestia of the hearth and fire ;

She would be useful if we wished to bake

Our bread at home.　Then Leto would aspire

To take her place not very far behind.

The mother of Apollo must be placed

As near as possible where she's inclined.

In this, good Boreas, you'll try and suit her taste.

Eternity, I think, would like some one

Of fibrous will to counsel her and serve her;

A sort of warrior without a gun.

We'll send an invitation to Minerva.

And, Ambofilius, there's a dame for you.

She knows your earth, her feet have kissed its

    floor.'

'Perhaps she'll take me back,' I said. 'Oh! do,

Pray, ask her when she can, if I'm a bore.'

'She's goddess of your green meats and your

    berries,

And decks her head with poppies and bright corn;

In Greece she's Demeter, in Rome she's Ceres,

She will my suite most charmingly adorn.

I don't know when she last went to your earth

Just ask her, Boreas, when she is going again.

'Tis not unlikely she might think it worth

Her while to take you back for some rich gain.'

'Rich gain, indeed!' I said. 'I shall not pay :

A goddess surely needs no such reward.

I'll be protector ; she can show the way,

That's all the payment that I can afford.'

Time smiled and said, ' Protector!' I smiled too.

'She needs no helmsman when she goes, my
       friend.

If either is to guard, she'll watch o'er you,

And see you safely to your journey's end.

Now, Boreas, are our noble guests complete;

Who is there more to make our list replete?

Great Æolus, of course, must find a place,

And if we take with us the big heroes,

Why should we not the smaller ones embrace?

There's Aphrodite's son, the wing'd Eros;

Then there's the great Apollo, god of song—

And Circe, Helios' daughter, with her arts.

The Muses we must have to swell the throng

And give a balance to the various parts.'

'Besides the men of courage there are shy men,'

Remarked Boreas, ' who no doubt will follow.

What say you to the handsome youth called

      Hymen,

Bearing his bridal torch, son of Apollo?'

'Follow, indeed! this boy must go in front!
The god of weddings, like the chaséd deer,
Must head the chasers and lead on the hunt,'
Said Time. 'See that his fiery torch burns clear.
While on your round, good Boreas, think of more.
There's threefold Hebe to close up the ranks.'

'If Morpheus comes,' I said, 'perhaps he'll snore,
And that would not incur your honour's thanks.'

'The son of sleep, my worthy friend, must be
The last of all,' said Time. 'He can preside
At drawing of the curtain, and just see
That both of us are well tucked up inside.'

'Well, then, if you achieve too much success,
You had better have the doctress Nemesis.'

'That's not a bad idea,' said Time.   'Oh! yes,

We'll have her with us on the premises.'

With this, as far as Boreas was concerned,

The conference closed. 'Now Boreas, good-bye,'

Said Time.   'When you have finished you'll

        have earned

The gratitude of yours faithfully.'

So Time and Ambofilius turned about

To near his home, when filling both their eyes

There came a brilliant pageant spreading out

Of his attendants, meaning to surprise

Their worshipped master with some choicer gifts.

The size of his success was now made known,

And one and all, as when some joy uplifts

In sudden bound the passive heart, had shown

Fresh-kindled eagerness to share with him

The pleasure he had captured for his heart.

So as Time turned he heard a joyful hymn

Spread out its harmony as all took part.

The fairy maidens of his household came,

Each nursing fondly in her shapely arms

The offspring of a thought born of his fame ;

Which, as they neared, they bore in open

      palms,

Smiling a prayer that he would kindly take

This tribute of their gratitude to him.

He took from all and said, for each one's sake

With pleasure he received, and to its brim

His heart responding filled with his best thanks.

Then mingling with the groups he spoke with all,

Nor failing in attention to all ranks,

Gave heed to every individual.

Dispersing slowly, some this way some that,

The company broke up, and Time retired.

'Come, Ambofilius, let us have a chat,

And see if our ideas can be inspired,'

He said. 'Eternity now thinks of me,

And wonders if the cunning of my mind,

With shuttle of device, weaves secretly

The plans I promised she in time should find

A fabric perfect for the critic's eye.

My embassy, whose chief is Boreas,

Is on the wing to summon hastily

My leading guests, and for this glorious

Occasion I must really find for you

A noble part. Say, Ambofilius!

If I bid you elect out of the few

Best places, be not so punctilious

As to choose the least.   Let me fix for you

A place with Æolus.   He is the power

Who dominates the winds.   With him the view

Would be immense and grand, as on a tower

You stood upon your earth sky high, to see

A flight of comets race ten million miles.

' I fear,' I said, ' god Æolus would be

Indignant to be charged with one who styles

Himself a denizen from Pluto's world.'

' I'll manage that,' said Time; 'you go with

    him.

Mind only, when his bound-up power's uncurled,

And you through endless space begin to skim,

You pay attention to the god's commands.

You are not provided with a pair of wings,

And so must keep in mind that he with hands

Is only safe from falling when he clings.'

' From falling ! thank you,' I remarked with awe,

' Could I hold on in one of his typhoons ?

My senses would disperse ; each clutching claw

Would merge its nature in nebulæ of high

      swoons.'

' That would indeed be a catastrophe,

The like of which we cannot contemplate,'

Said Time. ' We must from such disasters be

Too well protected, sir, at any rate.

With Æolus you'll have a foremost post

Well in the van, from which your searching eye

Can see the most distinguished of the host,

As they come sweeping through the blazing sky.

Time entered now with pensive look his home,

And thought, were he a scribe of facile pen,

He'd write an Iliad, and fill a tome

With deities and angels and real men.

' My friend,' he said, 'sharp turning on his heel,

I feel inspired with what I've seen and done.

When I unlock my memory, I feel

Such bursting forth, like Helios' blazing sun,

Of endless calendars of rarest sights

And panoramas of celestial deeds,

That, like your famous Homer, it delights

Me to loose out my brain, and while it bleeds

With heated images, dream in the past.

Can it be real, that I have found a wife ?

The thought of it is more than too divine.

I sometimes fear that I might lose my life

Before Eternity is really mine.

Oh, Ambofilius ! had you been with me

Up there in those bright regions far away ;

With me to know, to feel, to hear, to see

That it was true ; all true. That you could say

In words that I could hear and know were true,

That all those wonders were no fever'd dream.

My soul would then find rest.'

                ' To be with you.

When you were lost to us in that bright beam

Of heavenly light,' I said, ' was my desire.

I've never ceased to think of all you've said

About those heavenly regions in the skies.'

' 'Tis now too late,' said Time. ' When we are

    wed,

And gather flowers from our memories,

Perchance we shall be able to retrace

In company the paths which I have seen.

Eternity's all powerful to transplace

From lower to the higher realms, I ween.'

' Not such as I,' I said, ' dare ask her aid ;

Those regions are for men who've ceased to toil,

And have been ransomed to a higher grade ;

Who've slipp'd the mortal's chain, and cast its .

    coil.

Between my fixéd destiny, and there,

I see a gulf impassable to me

While I am mortal and know human care.

No, Time.   I'm not fit for Eternity.'

' Your judgment's wise, like all creation's laws ;

Your speech is purified in Reason's fire,'

He said. ''Tis true, there must be some such

    pause ;

Perhaps 'tis needed as a purifier.'

The same great hall that held us both before

Now closed around us with its cooling shades.

Just like a ship that's launchéd from the shore,

Time laid him down by slowly following

    grades.

He hailed a servitor, and bid him seek

Oceanus, and tell him to come in.

The captain came that we all three might speak

Of the great project—when it should begin.

Time said, ' Now, Ambofilius, let us hear

How weddings are conducted on your earth.'

'With pleasure,' I replied ; 'but I much fear

For you to know our ways is not much
    worth.'

'Indeed, my friend,' he said, ' I *wish* to know !

Wherever in this universe we live

The wisest of the wise can always learn.

In some things we must take, in others give ;

Each of us can the other help in turn.

Oratio veritatis simplex est.'

'Marriage,' I said, 'with us, begins man's
    serious life.

The course he then pursues will be the test,

And gauge his fitness to possess a wife.

Unmarried men, beyond a certain age,

Resemble tossing ships upon the sea

In search of shelter and sure anchorage ;

They are not happy, if they seem to be.'

' There's something human, then, in me,' said

     Time.

' For centuries my nature's had a thirst,

That fed upon me as a culprit's crime

Assails his mind, till it is near to burst.

A something in me grew that had no room.

My soul was like a heated cagéd plant,

That sucked its mother earth to make the bloom,

And fretted in its heart with fevered pant

To find the liberty that was denied.

'Tis thus that I've been prison'd and bereft

Of that for which my soul has vainly cried,

Like the frail lichen in the rock's dark cleft.

I've wandered up and down and through all space,

Just as a man whose brain has lost its root;

Nothing I heard or saw gave me solace.

Like a track'd deer the hunter sought to
>   shoot,

I've rushed about pursuing and pursued

To find a something that was nowhere found,

And followed as by panther for his food,

Stealthily nearing without show or sound.'

' What followed you ? '   Oceanus inquired.

' What *followed* me, Oceanus !   A thirst !

Like that would be if Helios, triple fired,

Dried up the waters in Poseidon's seas,

And left the fishes as by plague accursed

In their last plunging throe, scorched, murdered,
>   dead !'

' The deepest thirst Creation feels or sees

Is the devouring thirst of love,' I said.

' What Ambofilius says,' said Time, is true.

' Where blood is born to fill created veins

The blood breeds love.   Its richly purple blue

No power below or up in heaven restrains,

When male and female ripening fire the germs,

Which in them tremble, like a nervous hand,

Or noon-warm rosebuds   fighting with the

      worms,

Which eat the choicest shoots as they expand.

No, sirs, indeed, there's nothing even in heaven

Like that great sense.   It moves the deities !

On globes like that from which my friend is

      driven

It shakes great empires, and to me it is,

As I have said before, a new-born life.

My home in fact is now a little heaven.

Like one victorious in a deadly strife,

I rest content with that for which I've striven.'

'Well, now,' said Time, 'let my good people

    come.

We must have all things ready for the day

When fair Eternity will meet us.   Some

Can give their ear to what I have to say

Inside this hall ; but if no place is found

For all, then some must stay without and hear.

Give orders that my servitors go quickly round,

Oceanus, and bid our friends come here.

While they are gone, pray, Ambofilius, say

What are the customs in your much-loved land

When kings prepare a royal wedding-day ?'

' A great procession leaves the palace, and

Moves slow with stately march to music's sound.

A church, whose top is mantled in the clouds

Throws wide its doors, and spreading to the

     ground

Stream draperies of gold.   Excited crowds

Of loyal subjects line the course and cheer ;

While in the great cathedral may be seen

Archbishops, bishops, canons ; standing near

Are minor priests, the chapter, and the dean ;

Statesmen and heroes, writers, poets, wits ;

All who claim much renown, both young and old.

The church is full, the organ plays.   There sits

The king, emblazoned with his jewelled gold.

High raised upon a shining starry throne,

His head is crowned ; his countenance is grave;

In all the world there's no one more alone.

He's free ; but 'tis the freedom of a slave.'

'A king a slave!' said Time; 'how can that be?

He is the last of all to be enslaved.'

'Not bound with chains,' I said ; 'yet he's not

 free.

Upon the face of kings is deep engraved

The linkéd lines which have enchained their

 soul.

Like other mortals born to wealth and power,

They love to rule those whom they can control,

While life in them spins out its little hour.

A rumbling in the distance, like a storm,

Heralds the coming of the future queen.

Line after line, in military form,

Young, tall, and stalwart soldiers may be seen.

High raised in air the trumpet mouths declare

To him, who pale and patient sits and waits,

That she who fills his heart with loving care

Speeds on, and is without the church's gates.

Now louder music moves the quivering air,

And deep and full in measured time unrolls.

Ten thousand eyes converge on her and stare,

While brilliant banners, high on lifted poles,

Bend like the weeds that float upon the sea.

A surging cheer salutes her as she lights

Upon the soil of God's divinity,

The battle-field of man's religious fights.

A line of chosen courtiers now precedes

The lady's body-guard, whose gleaming dress,

Like brilliant flowers in frames of dusky weeds,

Lights up the mass of human nothingness.

The church is entered and the royal pair

Make vows to live in lasting continence.

A nation's praises rend the sacred air

As both in one are mergèd in permanence.

Rich gifts and wishes flow from every hand,

And all the world keeps festive holiday.

Loud allelujahs ring throughout the land

And lend magnificence to the display.'

My words thus ended ; and Time gently rose

And stroked his beard and looked about the
       ground.

' That is your finest pageant, I suppose ? '

Oceanus remarked, as he turned round.

''Tis well,' said Time; 'my friend has truly told.

What can be done with pageants must depend

Upon your means.   If they are rich and manifold

Processions once begun need never end.

My worthy friend knows well that on his sphere

The space and means are on a smaller scale.

My show will fill the skies ; the front and rear

Will look like fleets upon a sea, ten thousand sail.'

Time's servitors had now arrived in force,

And the Avenger rose and with loud voice

Bade all who could come in.   He said, the source

Of his great plans should partly be their choice.

' Oceanus, bring up your sailor men.

They've faced the dangers of the mighty deep

And we will see if they are paler when

They navigate the air with flightstrong leap.'

Oceanus stood up and said, 'Good sir !

My men, I'll wager, follow your lead.

In front of Poseidon not one would stir

When he was mad with rage and made them

    bleed.'

The multitude overflowed beyond the door,

And as Time rose the people's voices died

Down into nothing, as when rain will pour,

Then quickly stop, as if the heavens had dried.

' My friends,' he said, ' you are, I know, aware

That my lone life is coming to its end.

My vow has left the seed and in the air,

Like growing trees, its branches quick ascend.

My life begun when all things took their rise.

When first Diana spread her little arms

And met Aurora with her opening eyes

My own career begun.   The graceful charms

Of these fair twins my homage soon enthralled ;

Prudence so far has ruled my destiny.

But there's a time when each of us is called

By something, which like an epiphany,

His living soul close haunts with growing

    sense

Of some enslaved unsatisfied desire.

'Twas this that burned in me when I sailed

    hence,

Like an ungovernable raging fire.

It must have grown and spread for centuries,

Till such quintessence my soul so enslaved

That I pursued ideal effigies

Which my hot blood on my hot brain engraved.

My tortured soul at length its bondage burst,

And spread its wings to find a happier life.

If my poor fortune ended in the worst,

I still should only be without a wife.

I took a Hector's courage and set out;

My shibboleth was "*Jacta alea est.*"

Oceanus spreads sail, the sailors shout,

And full of hopes I steer out to the west.

My friends, the rest is like a story told;

A tale of wonder and high-brain'd romance,

Which I shall ne'er forget though I be old

By more than I am now, by twice, perchance.'

Time's hearers had sat mute as people dead,

So earnest were they listening to each thought;

That nothing might conflict with what he said,

Or hinder them from gaining what they sought.

Resuming his discourse, Time said, ' Well, now !

The time, my friends, is near when we shall meet

The fair Eternity, and my great vow

Will also near its end and be complete.'

At this the whole assembly, like a gale

Of new-born wind beam-ending some great ship,

Rose up, as if a fleet had spread each sail,

And shouted one and all a great hip ! hip !

Hip ! hip ! hip ! hip ! hurrah !   And then, again

They shouted hip ! hip ! hip ! hip ! hip ! hurrah !

With all their lungs and force and might and
     main,

Till echoes echoed echoes wide and far.

The crowd then broke and mingled, and the roar

Of their full voices heated in debate,

To those outside, resembled the great pour

Of some swift cataract precipitate

Down plunging many streams in headlong

   bound.

Time spoke with all ; but with a chosen few

Discussed the plans minutely, till they found

The object of this long-sought interview.

The gathering ended and they all dispersed,

The place of each appointed, and the day

When all should reassemble and be versed

Well in his rôle for Time's great wedding day.

The morning of the day selected dawned,

And Time, and all his suite, came forth prepared

All gaily decked and marshalled on the laund

Of his domain.   They showed that Time had

    cared

For the minutest wants of all his friends,

And perfect order reigned throughout his suite.

Like some great general a nation sends

To foreign lands with their commands, to treat

For peace or war as circumstances need,

Time close surveyed each one, that he might see

How far they were prepared for act and deed

Like that this day must end triumphantly.

While all were standing like an army drilled

To keep in perfect line prepared to fight,

The air changed colour and all round was filled

With darkness gently veiling o'er the light.

Beside Time stood his glass with running sand,

Which held his watchful eye as it ran out.

At length the grains were ended and his hand

Quick raised aloft showed all the whereabout

Of the descending host that blacked the sky.

To meet the leading gods Time spread his wings

And with him took a glance from every eye,

As subjects watch the movements of their kings.

The deities and their great suites came near,

Creating quite an artificial wind,

And making all the heavens around appear

As if their trains extended miles behind.

Then Æolus and Boreas and their suite

And all the Boreades lent their aid,

And raised Time's followers from their feet

Up level with the rest by gentle grade.

The gods and goddesses of highest rank

Now moved into the van of Time's great host,

And some came up behind till every blank

Was filled and each at his appointed post.

Then all was ready, and the hero of the day

Some distance on before took up his place,

And with a blast that shook the whole array,

And thundered forth their coming throughout

     space,

This mighty pageant pierced the trembling air.

The planets with their suns lit up the way

With treble flare ; the penetrating glare

Resembling all suns united for that day.

Diana and Aurora, close to Time,

Had burnished up their brightness to its best,

Which made the rays of Helios look like rime

Of dazzling silver, as they danced upon each

     breast.

Poseidon rode a cloud with wingéd steeds,

And made his trident breed electric light ;

His prancing horses filled with golden beads

The heavens around like bright stars in the
    night.

Dame Chaos in her sombre evening gown

Lent contrast to the corruscating glow

Of scintillating sparks, as they came down

From the commotion in its onward flow.

Apollo, with his glittering lyre, was heard

Above the roar of the displacéd air

Attuning his great choir, whose every word

Like choral thunder sounded everywhere.

To represent the Muses was Melpomene,

Whose tragic solos charmed the ears of all.

Urania came to personate astronomy ;

Polymnia, Thalia, Clio, and the tall

Erato stiffening Time's old ears to catch

The love-strains she spun from her fruitful
    brain.

The naughty poetess must even hatch

A little Cupid to enrich the strain.

Epic and lyric writing there must be

To make fit records of this great event.

Calliope epic, lyric Euterpe,

And there we have the Olympian contingent.

Great Zeus was there, and looking very studious,

As if he thought Time's scheme might interfere

With his position.   He called Pluvius,

And asked that god if he had aught to fear.

While Pluvius and the King of Heaven thus
>   spoke,

A blast from Boreas filled the air around.

The mighty host, as if from sleep awoke,

Seemed lifted by the thunder of the sound.

Straight out in front, as far as eye could reach,

A silvery dawn came creeping thro' the mist.

All eyes were strained to see, the ears of each

Were bended to the sound by lifted wrist.

Great silver beams and golden-coloured bars,

Like shining rays from Helios in the morn,

Spread through the heavens. Great star-
     decked golden cars,

By troops of wingéd gleaming angels drawn,

Came into view, refulgent with the quickening
     light ;

As if creation's suns had met to be,

Of all the features in that wondrous sight,

The one most pleasing to Eternity.

Time's soul now leaped within him, and he said

In silent speech, ' The angel of my life !

She comes ! she really comes ! The fearful dread

That she might not perhaps become my wife

Slow drags its awful weight from off my brain,

As my eyes reap this harvest for my soul.'

His eyes kept fixed upon the golden plain

Which looked like gleaming rivers as they roll

Straight out from many suns in one great

     stream.

Time raised his hands and said aloud to me,—

'Oh ! Ambofilius, I know *now* 'tis no dream ;

I see her coming ! Fair Eternity !'

The van of her great train now clearer shone

Against the brilliant heavens, distinctly seen.

Far up above the rest she sat upon

A crystal throne, a matchless heavenly queen.

All round her was a nimbus of fair forms ;

Great flights of angels soared above her head,

And far behind in endless, countless swarms

The train of her angelic followers spread.

The willing ears of all detect afar

The stronger sounds of murmuring harmony,

Which, as each second, like a falling star,

Throws down its life, breathes their antiphony

To purify and bathe the nuptial air

In which these mighty hosts shall celebrate

        that day,

The union of this high-born heavenly pair.

The heavens all round are now ablaze and gay

With stars in clusters, moons and suns in

        pairs.

The vault above is striped with dazzling hues,

Whose sparkling radiance every object shares,

While all around are wide enchanting views.

The hosts now halt, and in extended rows,

The gods and goddesses in front, the rest be-

    hind.

Like mountain ranges tipped with silver snows,

Peak after living peak aloft enshrined

In amber purity of sun's full ray.

Eternity's great suite in equal line

Then bounds the plain, dividing each array,

To which the tiers in gentle slope decline.

The leading personages on each side

Now leave their friends, and in the open meet

For salutation, and that they may guide

In their due course the functions of each suite.

Apollo's son the handsome Hymen sings

Alone, a strain as signal to the choirs,

Who poised aloft upon their outstretched wings

O'erarch with harmony the living spires.

Beneath is raised a dual nuptial throne,

With altar flanked by chosen cherubims.

All being ready, Time comes forth alone,

His advent heralded by martial hymns.

Then sweeter strains float on the golden air,

And shielded by a favoured few is seen

The fairer half of this illustrious pair,

Eternity, the chaste celestial queen.

Then Helios and his kin stir up their fires,

And all the minor lights shed stronger rays;

Resounding harmonies from all the choirs

With thunder stream to heaven in fullest praise

As they are joined by solemn marriage tie.

The potent Æolus and Boreas blow

Their tempered winds to spread throughout the

    sky

The allelujahs, as in force they grow.

The gods and goddesses with choicest gifts

Crowd round Eternity ; and happy Time

In unfeigned ecstasies his hands uplifts,

Moved by a sense of joy in him sublime.

Great Jupiter loud thunders throughout space

And rolls far off his massive monotone,

Sounding as if the planets in a race

Struck each the other till one ran alone.

To vary the full glow of Helios' light,

And match the thunder of great Zeus's lungs,

God Fulminator sent with peerless flight

His lightning through the heavens with shoot-

    ing tongues.

Then Pluvius, to cool down the burning sky

And let his gentle rain the sunbeams kiss,

The water frees, o'erarching splendidly

With coloured bows these realms of perfect bliss.

Minerva, with Poseidon hand in hand,

Congratulate with smiles the married pair ;

While Venus and fair Juno with their band

Of followers their homage deep declare.

Time now assists Eternity to rise

And take the throne intended for his bride,

While he the other proudly occupies

Sweet smiling on his consort by his side.

The great united hosts then change their place,

And marshal all their strength before the thrones.

The gods in front with Time are face to face,

A peerless gathering he frankly owns.

The King of Heaven great Jupiter and Zeus,

When silence held full undisputed sway,

Rose up ; and that he might on them produce

Impression deep, close bordering on dismay,

He let his thunder roar loud peal on peal

Till all the air was heaving like a sea

Cast from a storm's embrace, and made to reel

Like the carouser from his revelry.

Then with proud mien and elevated head

In measured phrase, deliberate, he said,--

' Eternity, great Time, the gods, and men !

The heavens bear witness that the deed is
   done.

Two mighty powers are joined, and you,
   Hymen,

Should make your torch like Helios' brightest
   sun

Shed its clear lustre through infinite space.

Let god Pluto his largest planet spare

And there it fix, that every coming race

May see it burn, and know that it was there

On that illustrious spot where you now
stand,

And where this great assembly looks on me,

That she in marriage gave to Time her hand,

The beauteous goddess, chaste Eternity!

This grand event, my noble sires and dames,

Illumes creation's history with a sun

Which lights for ever, on its roll, the names

Of Time and of Eternity in one.

In great Creation's name I raise my voice,

For you and me, to wish them happiness;

Inspire your choirs, Apollo, and rejoice

In hymns and songs of heavenly loveliness;

So swell your chant that all in heaven may
hear,

And their best choirs in fullest song employ.

Now shake the universe with one great
cheer,

And wish our wedded friends much joy.'

THE END.

COLSTON AND SON, PRINTERS, EDINBURGH.